Full Circle

*Book Three
of the
Juniata Iron Trilogy*

Dillsburg Area Public Library
204 A Mumper Lane
Dillsburg, PA 17019
717-432-5613

Judith Redline Coopey

Full Circle

Copyright 2016, Judith Redline Coopey
All rights reserved.
Print ISBN: 978–0-9838918–0-2
All E-book editions: 978–0-9838918–1-9

This is a work of fiction. Any resemblance to persons, living or dead, is purely coincidental. No part of this book may be reproduced or transmitted in any form or by any means, electronic or mechanical, including photocopying, recording, or by an information storage and retrieval system—except by a reviewer who may quote brief passages in a review to be printed in a magazine or newspaper or on the Worldwide Web—without permission in writing from the publisher. For information, please contact Fox Hollow Press, 1725 North Sundial, Mesa, Arizona 85205.

Interior design by OPA Author Services, Scottsdale, Arizona
Cover design by John M. Coopey, Mesa, Arizona

ATTENTION CORPORATIONS, UNIVERSITIES, COLLEGES, AND PROFESSIONAL ORGANIZATIONS: Quantity discounts are available on bulk purchases of this book for educational or gift purposes, or as premiums for increasing magazine subscriptions or renewals. Special books or book excerpts can also be created to fit specific needs. Contact Fox Hollow Press.

FOX HOLLOW
PRESS

Digitally printed in the United States of America

Dedication

For Helen Roller

Acknowledgments

As I've worked my way through this trilogy, a number of people have come to the fore, bringing encouragement, expertise and supporting my research. I thank all those who gave of their time, energy and knowledge to broaden my understanding of the iron industry and Mt. Etna.

The list could go on and on, but I especially thank Gary Discavage, Dorothy Koontz, Cheryl Hughes, John Roller and Dan Detweiler. Then, too, I thank my ever stalwart preliminary readers, Mary Agliardo, Erin Coopey, Pamela Leipold and Pat Park, and my indispensable editor, Paul McNeese.

Chapter 1

Sarah, 1901

Sitting in a lawn chair, reading and daydreaming on a sultry August afternoon, my reverie was interrupted by an insulting clatter and the insistent blaring of some metallic-sounding horn. I pulled myself up taller and peered over my reading glasses to see what invader was bringing dread upon us. A motor car! A funny little horseless carriage, huffing and chuffing its way along the road, bearing two duster-clad occupants and sending chickens and dogs into terrified flight. Well, who would have thought Mt. Etna would ever see one of these infernal machines come to devour and leave us in its dust?

The clatter brought my brothers running from different directions—Ned from the riverbank where he'd been fishing—what else?—and Andrew from the stable, where he'd been carefully grooming a handsome chestnut gelding, newly purchased from a neighbor.

"Wow! What's that?" Ned cried, in the excitement of the moment. He stood by the road, starry eyed, open mouthed, amazed.

"That, little brother, is a motor car!" Andrew stood with his arms crossed, watching the strange little machine huff and chuff its way past the manor house and on toward the mill. Then it stopped. Not like it'd stopped at the driver's command, just stopped of its own accord.

"Come on, Ned, let's go see it." Andrew was already running toward the mill, his thick, dark hair rising and falling to the rhythm of his pace. I thought I'd stay and get back to my book, but before long the whole village was turning out to see this miracle of modern technology, so I left my book and my glasses and walked, lady-like and sedate, down to join the oohs and ahhs.

A horseless carriage, painted red with gold pin stripes, its varnished, wooden wheels covered with dust, stood helpless beside the mill. Andrew and Ned were already engaged with the driver, a man of considerable age to be gadding about in a hell machine like that, and the other occupant, who looked young enough to be his daughter. Turned out we knew them—or knew *of* them, at least. Not that we were impressed by this conspicuous display of wealth—not I, at least.

Richard Trethaway came out of the mill, dusting flour off his apron, and joined the admiring crowd. He waved to me and I waved back before we both turned our attention to the attraction.

"Michael Judge—from Huntingdon." The man extended a gloved hand to Andrew, then thought better and took the glove off, along with a pair of goggles that left a clean circle amid the dust around each eye. Andrew shook his hand and stepped back, hands in his pockets, more interested in the flivver—that's what he called it, a flivver—than in the young woman who had hopped down and was now smiling up at him as though renewing an old acquaintance.

"Fine machine. How long have you had it?"

Michael Judge took off his other glove and nodded to me as he lifted the metal cover on the motor. He stuck his head inside, reached here and there, twisted this, tinkered with that and turned back to the onlookers. Bending over a right angled crank, he gave it a turn and stepped back. The motor coughed, sputtered, and died again.

The girl was his daughter, Bertha, a sometime fellow student of mine at Juniata College in Huntingdon, though I wouldn't have called us friends. Bert, as she was known, had a reputation as a spoiled rich girl, used to getting what she wanted. I watched her maneuver around my handsome, West Point graduate brother, hoping he had sense enough to resist her rather obvious efforts to engage him.

Richard stood by, taking in the scene, not missing a thing. A keen observer of the human condition, he would take note and discuss it all with us later. Richard's observations entertained and informed. For a common miller, he could discern motive and attitude as well as any student of behavior, and his conclusions were right on. He stood watching the goings on, eyes on Michael Judge, then Bert, then Andrew. I anticipated a good analysis later in the day.

"Must take a lot to keep that thing running." Completely forgetting his ever present shyness around strangers, Ned circled the little contraption, arms crossed. His observation was met with a frown from Mr. Judge.

"Not really. Just a little encouragement now and then." He turned to Andrew, pride in his stance. "Just got it last week. First in Huntingdon. Still learning its quirks. Cost me a pretty penny, I can tell you."

Andrew stood back, looking thoughtful. "Seems like you'd wait until they're more reliable, though. What will you do if you can't get it started again?"

"Leave her right here until I can get a mechanic to take a look."

"Leave her? Really?"

"Yep. Leave her right here. Nobody's going to steal her, that's for sure. Wouldn't know how to drive her if she *would* go."

Ned continued to circle the vehicle, peering at it from every angle, charmed. "Sure is pretty," he said.

I marveled at how at ease he was, engaging in conversation with a stranger as if it was what he did every day. Ned was painfully shy, tended to avoid contact with strangers at any cost, and when forced to engage, might as likely run away as exchange a greeting.

"Well, do you think you'll get her running again?" It was clear Andrew wanted to get his head under that hood and tinker. Mr. Judge, sensing that, moved aside to let him look.

"It's a two stroke engine," Andrew told us over his shoulder. "Pretty simple. Should be easy to set her to rights."

The village folk, along with Ned and I watched as Andrew loosened this and tightened that, then stepped back, wiping his hands on a rag from the car's rear compartment.

He nodded to Michael Judge. "Crank her up."

Bert Judge edged closer to Andrew, took off her cap and goggles and fluffed her hair. Watching her obvious efforts to gain his attention piqued my proprietary rights as a sister.

As Mr. Judge bent over the crank, a palpable air of expectation hovered over the crowd. One turn. Two turns. Three turns—and the engine sputtered to life.

"There you go," Andrew smiled. "Want me to ride back with you, just in case? I could follow on horseback."

Bert brightened at that idea, but Michael Judge shook his head. "Naw. I'll be all right. Show me what you did, in case it dies on me again."

Andrew obliged, and the two men spent another ten minutes discussing the workings of the motor while the village folk, reminded that they had other things to do, wandered away. Bert sidled over and greeted me as though she'd just realized who I was. "Sarah! Sarah MacPhail! How nice to see you. I didn't know you lived out here. Really, this is a lovely place. Old iron works, my daddy says."

All the while she was talking to me her eyes were darting back and forth between me and Andrew. "Who's *this* fellow and where did he learn so much about motor cars?"

"He's my brother, Andrew." I resolved to dispense as little information as possible, aware that she was collecting it for her own purposes. I stayed on, talking to Tess Gorman, an old family friend who lived in the little house up Roaring Run Hollow

"See Ned's curious about that horseless carriage," Tess observed, nodding toward my younger brother. "Forgot his shyness."

I nodded. "It'll be back as soon as he remembers he hasn't known Mr. Judge all his life."

"Think he's maybe outgrowing it?"

"It" was a strange personality quirk that made Ned, sixteen now, taciturn, distant and socially inept. I was used to his backward ways—indeed, all of Mt. Etna was, but to anyone new he'd seem strange, if not outright odd.

I sighed. "No, not really. He's just forgotten himself for a moment. The fright'll be back." All the while I talked to Tess, I kept an eye on Bert, maneuvering to stay close to Andrew.

Tess reached out and patted my shoulder. "Shame for such a handsome lad. He always was the pet of your dad."

"Yes. Sometimes I think Mama and Papa spoiled him. Let him have his way too much. You know, coddled him so he didn't have to work out his problems."

The clank of the metal motor cover signaled the end of the afternoon interlude, so I took my leave of Tess, reminded of my responsibilities as a hostess.

"Mr. Judge, would you come to the manor house for tea?" I really hoped he'd say no—that they'd be on their way and that Bert wouldn't have a chance to get her talons into my brother, but Mr. Judge hesitated, then smiled.

"I'm not sure I'd be welcome in your mother's home. I'm the same Michael Judge as bought a lot of land from your father before he died. That's why I came up here. To look over a parcel I've sold to a stone company. I know how your family hates selling off land, especially to speculators like me."

Anxious to save our reputation for hospitality, Andrew stepped up and rescued me. "Nonsense, Mr. Judge. A deal is a deal. Our mother would welcome you like any other guest. Come on, you must be thirsty after driving around in the dust."

So the Judges joined us on the front porch of the manor house, where Mrs. Beck, our "new" cook—she'd only been with us for twenty years, as opposed to the old cook, Mrs. Gwynn, who'd been with us for forty—served up a delightful tea, with fresh strawberries and cream on a dainty little shell of a cake.

I helped my mother play the hostess, pouring tea and offering second helpings, while Bert took every advantage in her quest to get acquainted with Andrew. She smiled, looked up from under her eyelashes while demurring at the offer of seconds, playing the coy ingénue to a tee.

Andrew, oblivious to the charms so boldly displayed, addressed her father. "So, Mr. Judge, your name *is* familiar. I think I heard my father speak of you."

"Yes, you probably did. My father, Timothy Judge, worked the store over at Yellow Spring way back. We lived there when I was a boy. The less said about that, the better, though."

Andrew looked questioning, but Mr. Judge carried the conversation on to other things. He looked at me. "You and Bert should strike up a friendship."

I smiled and nodded. "We're already acquainted. We were in classes together at Juniata last term."

Mr. Judge smiled "Oh, then you know each other. How nice."

"We're just getting ready to take me back to school tomorrow."

He nodded. "Bert was in Pittsburgh last week, shopping for her fall wardrobe. That girl will put me in the poorhouse yet." Spoken with a certain pride.

I smiled again, watching his daughter, a tiny wren full of energy and sauciness, concentrate her attention on my brother. Not a favorite with me, she was known campus-wide as a sassy little chippie, and the talk was that she was 'fast'.

Michael Judge pushed his chair back from the table and smiled in fatherly indulgence. "Yes, I'm afraid my daughter's not the saint her late mother was. Sometimes I think she doesn't know where the boundaries are, and sometimes I think she just doesn't care." He laughed loud, slapped his knee and rose, looking around at the company with fatherly pride. "I guess that's what comes of being an only child to an aging father. She tells me I shouldn't be driving this motor car. Says it should be hers. Well, one day it will be, but not yet a while."

Bert, pert and impertinent, played the shy daughter to his proud parent.

"We'd best be going. Want to get back to town before dark." Michael Judge nodded to our mother and me, shook Andrew's hand and clapped Ned on the shoulder. "Pleasure meeting you, folks. You'll be seeing some activity along the river, downstream a ways. I've sold that quarry over on Tussey to a limestone company. They plan on developing it now that the railroad spur is in and reliable. Plan on building a whole town to house the workers."

With that bit of tantalizing news, Michael Judge and his daughter departed, leaving us to wonder just what kind of change was in store.

I went down the steps into the yard to pick up my book and spectacles, found the book where I'd left it, but the spectacles lay on the ground, stepped on, both lenses shattered.

"Ned! I shrieked. "Ned MacPhail, you come down here right this minute. Did you do this?" I held the broken glasses out to him.

"No." He shook his head. "Why do you think I did?"

"Because you're such an oaf, Ned. You probably stepped on them and didn't even notice. How will I ever get another pair before classes start?" Extremely far-sighted, I needed my glasses for practically everything I did—reading, needlework, even following a recipe. I knew they made me look owlish—little round lenses in black wire frames with flimsy J-shaped hooks wrapping around my ears, but hyperopia was my lot, and I simply couldn't get along without them.

Ned stood by, protesting his innocence.

"It's all right, Ned. I know you didn't mean to." I carried the empty frames into the house, wrapped them in my handkerchief, and deposited them on a side table in the hallway. No more reading for me until I could get another pair. I sighed.

Then it occurred to me that Ned was telling the truth. In fact, I knew he was. Ned never lied. Every thought, every opinion, every observation that Ned shared with anyone was dead-on honest. Flustered by regret for having accused him and then disbelieved him, I went back out on the porch, where he was intent on tying a hook on a fishing line, and gave him a hug.

"I'm sorry, Ned. I don't know what happened to the glasses, but if you say it wasn't you, I believe you."

"It was you, Sarie. You did it yourself. I saw you. When you got up to go see the motor car, you dumped them out of your lap and stepped on them."

"Oh. Well, why didn't you just say so?"

He picked up his cap from the porch banister, plopped it on his curly blond head and went down the steps into the yard. "Because you get so much kick out of bossing me around, I thought I'd just let you have your fun."

Chapter 2

Richard, 1901

The good thing about living around here is that nothing ever changes. The trouble with living around here is that nothing ever changes. I guess that's what you get when you live on what's left of a hundred-year-old iron plantation thirty years after iron has gone to rust. Not that I'd ever want to live anywhere else. Born here, grew up here, probably die here. Oh, I'm nowhere near that. I'm only twenty-four, but I already know my life is here.

I'm not complaining, though. There are other places, other lives, but I'm just one of those easy going folk that don't yearn for much more than they have. My grandfather, Jude Trethaway was like that. He left once to go fight in the War Between the States, but he came back and never felt the need to leave again. Some folks just can't get away far enough or fast enough—or find enough adventure to hold them, but not me.

Take Sarah MacPhail, the last Iron Master's daughter. She still lives in the big house, even though they've had to sell off a lot of land and will probably have to sell more. But Sarah's gone off to Juniata College in Huntingdon, looking for something she thinks ain't here.

Full Circle

My pa, James Trethaway, ran the mill at Mt. Etna. My grandpa Jude ran it before him, and my great grandpa Jeff Baker ran it before that. I run it now, but there's hardly enough business to keep it runnin.' I like milling, so I'm good for stayin' here. Continuity's a good thing—one generation to the next. I guess there'd still be a MacPhail runnin' the furnace if there was anything left of the iron business.

Me and Sarah grew up alongside, but ever since she's gone off to college, her head's been turned. I'm afraid she's going to meet some college boy and get married and move away—sell the whole caboodle. That'd be a sorry day for me.

Her pa, Laird MacPhail, a good man, died last year. He ran the iron business as long as he could, but even he could see there was no future in small iron furnaces. They'd had their day, though. Time was when Juniata Iron was the finest anywhere, and the packet boats on the canal hauled tons of it to the Portage Railroad in Hollidaysburg and up over the mountain to Johnstown and Pittsburgh. Time was when Mt. Etna bustled with the activity of producing Juniata Iron, with ore mines, quarries, charcoal burning, iron smelting going on day and night. That was before my time, but I've heard enough about it to know it was a bustling place back about fifty years.

Now it's quiet, peaceful, bordering on poor. Folks don't want to live here anymore. No reason to, unless, like me, you're born to it. Lots of things going on in Altoona, where the railroad shops go like Mt. Etna used to—jobs and places to go, things to see. They've got a park there at Lakemont that has all the attractions you could think of. Picnic tables and rides and a lake with boats. They've even got a roller coaster—Leap the Dips—that goes so fast it makes your hair stand on end. Or so they say. I've never been.

So I guess I'll stay here and keep the mill runnin'—'cause I'm not inclined to adventure or travel. I'll leave that to Sarah's brother Andrew, in the Army for life. His orders will be comin' soon and he'll be gone. Then there's Sarah, going to college, sure to get married and move on. That leaves Ned and his mother, Miss Anna. She's a lot younger than her husband was, so I guess she'll stay here and take care of Ned.

See, Ned's kind of backward, you might say. He's real shy—won't talk to strangers—won't even look at them. He'd cross the road or cross the river to keep from having to talk to one. He's all right at home and with us Mt. Etna folk, except that he talks about fish and fishing all the time. Some folks think he's a little queer 'cause that's all he talks about. Fish and fishing. He can tell you everything about a fish—what kind it is, what kind of water it likes, what it likes to eat, everything. He keeps records of every fish he catches—draws pictures of them, puts down how big they are and what day he caught them and where and what kind of bait he was using. He already has a bunch of notebooks full of his fish pictures. So I don't think Ned will be going anywhere far away, like Andrew and Sarah. He'll probably just live here with his mother and fish all his life.

Andrew's taking Sarah back to Huntingdon tomorrow for the fall term at Juniata. She's all excited. It's her third year, and she's real anxious to get back to school. I'll go over this evening and help Andrew load her trunks and boxes. They'll go in the little shay and I'll follow with the wagon.

Sarah

Andrew drove me down to Huntingdon in the shay, followed by Richard Trethaway with the wagon, my boxes and trunks piled high and tied down. Andrew was happy to accompany me back to college, always on the lookout for a smart and pretty girl. There are lots of them at Juniata. Actually, I had a plan for Andrew. It involved my roommate of two years, Claire Butler from Lewistown, a dark-haired, blue-eyed beauty, the perfect mate for my soldier brother, seated tall and straight beside me, holding the reins with authority.

As we drove up in front of Founder's Hall to complete my registration and get my class schedule, Claire and her father drove up from the opposite direction.

"Claire! Hello! Claire!" I rose from the seat and waved vigorously, intent upon catching her attention so she wouldn't miss seeing Andrew in the splendor of his Army uniform. She saw me and returned my wave, her face full of the joy of reunion.

"How was your summer?" I asked, alighting from the shay almost before it came to a stop.

Claire ran up and embraced me, her eyes trained on Andrew. "Oh, yes. Claire, this is my brother, Lieutenant Andrew MacPhail. You've heard me speak of him."

"Heard of him! I've heard of little else *but* him since I've known you. Really, Sarah, you shouldn't have kept him away so long!" Claire walked right up to Andrew and offered her hand, no shrinking violet, she. Then, turning to me, she asked, "Did you get our room assignment? I hope it's the same old room at Mrs. Wright's. I've come to love it as much as home."

Andrew, normally straight and sober, opened a broad smile for Claire and immediately bowed and kissed her hand as though she were a French heiress. Clearly taken with her, he turned to her father and asked directions to our rooming house. Mr. Butler responded with a wave of his arm, returned to his rig, and led the way down Moore Street to Sixteenth where he turned right and continued down to the middle of the block.

Claire and I followed on foot, busily chattering about our summer and our fall classes. By the time we got to the big, brick house set back from the street, Andrew and Richard had already begun carrying trunks, valises, boxes and bags up the front steps. We girls rushed up to the third floor to oversee the placement of everything, full of chatter and excitement at the prospect of the new term.

Mrs. Wright, our landlady, stood by in good humor, showing the men where to put things and directing the deposit of the empty trunks and packing boxes in the basement. Widowed, Mrs. Wright made her way by renting out the top two floors of her home to students, young ladies all, from Juniata College. Claire and I occupied the third floor, while three rooms on the second were let to girls from Altoona, Tyrone and Phillipsburg. The gracious lady provided us with breakfast each morning and a neat little sack lunch if our schedule prohibited return to her table for the mid-day meal. Dinner was served promptly at six, followed by devotions, study and bedtime. Lights out at ten P.M.

The unpacking and rearranging took the better part of three hours, so when we were finished, it was drawing near to dinner time. I did so want Andrew and Claire to get to know one another. Claire's father, a dry goods merchant, had a longer drive home than Andrew did, so he left his daughter in our care and set out for Lewistown around four o'clock.

Richard waved to me from his wagon seat. "I'm for home, too, then," he said, mustering a wry smile. It always made Richard sad when I left. I guess he thought since Mt. Etna was now so tiny, the absence of one single person made all the difference. Tall and good-looking in an unpretentious way, Richard was as familiar to me as the old furnace itself. Always there.

"Good-bye, Richard. I'll see you for Thanksgiving!"

With a nod, he drove off down Moore Street, handling the team with authority, heading home.

Andrew offered to take Claire and me downtown to the Franklin House for dinner, a prospect that met with Claire's hearty approval. On the way, we stopped at the optical offices of Dr. Theron McDonald and dropped off my sad, shattered glasses. Dr. McDonald promised they'd be repaired by the middle of the next week. I shuddered. That meant almost a week of classes before I'd be able to read my first assignments.

At the Franklin House we were seated at a lovely table by the window, where we could watch the trains come and go from the Huntingdon depot. Claire and I chattered amiably throughout the meal, with Andrew adding a certain military charm to the proceedings. I was sure Claire would be taken with him, handsome and accomplished as he was.

"Andrew, tell us about the Army. Where do you think you'll serve?" She leaned in close, hands clasped, elbows on the table, looking into his eyes.

Andrew smiled, more than happy to talk about the Army, especially to one so charming and attentive as Claire. "I've orders for San Francisco, California—at the Presidio, probably for at least six years. Then who knows? Could be anywhere in the country—or abroad, I suppose. Maybe the Philippines. We have forces there, you know."

Claire's expression darkened at that bit of news. "The Philippines? How could you stand to be so far away?"

"Oh, I wouldn't mind. I'd be kept busy with my duties and learning Spanish. A soldier goes where he's sent and does the bidding of his superiors."

"But the Philippines? Really? Surely you can get yourself assigned somewhere in the good old United States."

Andrew smiled. "I'll serve where the Army sends me. Duty, honor, country, you know."

My hopes for matchmaking began to ebb, for Andrew was already married to the military, and any woman who sought to share his life would have to honor that commitment. Claire, on the other hand, was interested only in what was new and popular, and that only for the moment. But still there seemed a spark between them, and I nurtured my hopes.

A sprightly little shay, pulled by a trim young mare, drove up on the cobbles as we left the Franklin House, and who should alight but yesterday's guest, Bert Judge. She stopped and greeted us again as though we were the best of friends, her eye unwavering on Andrew even as she gushed over Claire's dress and complimented my hat.

"How is our military friend?" she asked in a casual tone, grasping Andrew's hand in both of hers. She looked into his eyes and said, "The United States Army! My, my, how impressive!"

That must have piqued Claire, for she reached out and tucked her hand around Andrew's arm. "Yes, he is, isn't he?" she laughed. "Come, Andrew, we really must be going. Sarah looks tired."

Bert stepped back and let us pass, her eyes never leaving Andrew's face, a look of bold admiration following him to the shay. "Nice to meet you, Lieutenant. Maybe you'll come down for a visit sometime and we can get to know each other."

Bold as brass. No discretion. No decorum. Just blatant audacity. Humph.

Back in our room that evening, I dismissed Bert Judge from my consciousness, anxious to hear about Claire's summer. As usual, she'd had a delightful time, traveling almost every weekend, visiting with friends and attending weddings, planning parties and breaking hearts.

"Oh, Sarah, you should have been in Harrisburg with us. We had a party on the island right in the middle of the river—had it all to ourselves. Everyone was there. Then Wells Nearhoof invited me to spend a week—a whole week—at his sister's house on Long Island. Long Island, Sarah! Have you ever been?"

I shook my head. Claire's life was so much more exciting than mine. She knew everybody, was friends with most and intimate with quite a few—commanding the spotlight wherever she went. Grateful to tag along in Claire's shadow, the little girl with the owlish glasses, I hoped some—just a little—of her charm might rub off on me. .

Oh, we were friends—close and loving friends who shared almost everything. Almost. There was something I'd never told Claire. A secret so monumental as to be kept from all the world. I was in love. Claire knew him, too. Indeed everyone at Juniata knew him, for he was one of our instructors, Phillip Chamberlain. I'd been in love with him since the first day I set foot in his classroom as a freshman, enthralled by his readings of poetry and intimate knowledge of all the English poets and their work. Mr. Chamberlain—he wasn't Doctor Chamberlain yet—introduced me to the stimulating world of romantic poetry. Keats, Shelley, Byron. Ahh, life! Ahh, love!

So I was waiting with little patience for classes to begin again so I could spend my allotted three hours per week in the presence of my Adonis. I'd taken every class he taught, the great poets claiming my undying devotion. I'd even written some poetry myself and shyly presented it to Mr. Chamberlain at the end of last term. He'd read it and praised me highly, smiled at me and even touched my arm. I'd barely been able to abide spending three whole months away from him. This term I'd get up the courage to show him more of my work and perhaps even invite him to Mt. Etna for a weekend visit.

So this evening I was set on the path to reveal my secret to Claire, but something in her demeanor made me hesitate, for she was deep into telling me all about her summer—her crushes, her adventures, her raptures. It was ever thus with Claire. No back and forth. No fair exchange of tales, hopes, dreams. Everything was about Claire and her life. And yet I still enjoyed her—loved her, really—for she was everything I longed to be.

I listened as she went on and on about her suitors. It seemed every eligible bachelor for miles around was lined up for her hand, but she was holding out for something better. Always something better. I wondered at her expectation that her life would be a continuous mix of romance and adventure, but, of course, I'd never mention such doubt. My secret withstood the endless tales about Claire Butler's social life. We talked until well after lights out and continued in muffled voices until after eleven.

By that time, I was ready for sleep, so I put my secret away for another day.

Chapter 3

Richard, 1901

After I dropped Sarah off at the college, I drove down to Penn Street and stopped for a glass of beer at the Standing Stone Tavern. I stopped there some and usually met someone I knew, so I pulled a chair over to a table near the door and watched for a familiar face. One arrived, in the person of my cousin, Daniel Trethaway, a favorite with me. "Evening, Daniel."

"Evening, Richard. What brings you down this way of an evening?"

"Brought Sarah back to college."

"Ah, yes. Juniata. Does she like it there, do you think?"

"Oh, yes. My guess is she'll find a husband and be gone before long."

Daniel smiled and nodded. "Most likely. And what of her brother, Ned? How's he faring since his father died?"

"As you'd expect. He doesn't show emotion, though. Just goes along as usual, fishing. His mother will be caring for him for some time, I think."

"Too bad. He's always seemed . . . a little odd."

"Depends on what you mean by odd. Ned's smart and even witty at home. He's just a little shy—doesn't fit in with people he doesn't know."

Daniel sipped his beer, peering at me over his glass. I didn't expect him to see Ned as I did. Most people didn't, but I always thought Ned'd be all right some day, given time.

Outside, a new-looking shay passed along the tree-shaded street, pulled by the neatest little mare I'd seen in a while. "Will you look at that?" I exclaimed.

"What?"

"That mare would win first at anybody's fair."

Daniel leaned forward to look out the door. "Oh, that. That's Michael Judge's daughter, Bert. Naughty little thing, but she knows her horse flesh. Saw that mare on a farm down near Bellville and insisted her father buy it for her."

"Oh, funny. They were just up at Mt. Etna yesterday driving a motor car."

"Oh, yeah, that'd be Mike Judge. Gotta have the best new thing, no matter the cost. I guess he can afford it, though. Money just seems to come to him."

The shay did a neat u-turn and stopped across the street from the tavern. I rose and stepped out to get a better look at the little mare. Bert hopped down, smiling in recognition.

"Didn't I see you up at Mt. Etna yesterday?" she asked with a sidelong glance, running a hand down the horse's foreleg.

"Yes, I'm the miller up there. Richard Trethaway. Nice horse."

She smiled, her blue eyes fluttering. "My favorite. She's fast, too." She looked me up and down with a sideways glance. It occurred to me that she must flirt with every man she met. I didn't mind.

"So where's your heart, with horses or motor cars?"

"Oh, horses, to be sure. Motor cars are exciting, but you can love a horse and it loves you back."

"Atta girl. My kind of woman. Don't let your head be turned by modernity," I laughed.

Again the fluttering eyes. "I'll have to ride up to Mt. Etna some time and we can ride together—if you have a fast horse, that is."

"Got one that'd run your little mare ragged in a quarter mile."

She turned and hopped back up onto the shay, clucked to her horse and walked her, calm and sedate, back the way she'd come. "We'll have to see about that!" she called over her shoulder as she drove away.

I returned to Daniel, who was leaning back in his chair, thumbs in his pants pockets. "I'd watch out for that one, Richard. She just might beat you in that race." He took a drink of beer. "What else is new?" he asked.

"Looks like Michael Judge has sold that land he bought across the river from Mt. Etna. Quarrying company. Moving right along. Brought in a rock crusher already. Even starting to build housing for the workers. A whole town."

"Yes, I've heard some talk about it. Didn't he buy that land from Laird MacPhail? Probably doubled his price already. Anyway, it might spark things up at Mt. Etna to have new folks coming in. I hear they're gonna call the town Blair Four. Don't know where they came up with that name." Daniel leaned back in his chair, stretching his legs out long in front of him.

"I do. There were four locks on the old canal right near there. Can't say I'm excited about it, though. Change can be for the good or not. I kind of like things the way they are."

A loud laugh escaped my cousin. "You're an old man, Richard. You were born an old man, and you're an old man at twenty-four. Wonder what you'll be like in another forty years!"

I laughed, too, comfortable with the label. Old Man Trethaway. I could live with that.

Chapter 4

Sarah, 1901

So when classes began the next morning, I was there early, standing outside Mr. Chamberlain's assigned classroom in Founder's Hall, breathing heavy and trying to slow my racing heart. He walked up the stairs and turned to face me, flashing an easy smile.

"Good morning, Miss MacPhail. How nice to see you again. How was your summer?"

I smiled back, then looked down. Unseemly to be too forward. "Quite nice, really. I read a lot and wrote some."

"Where are your spectacles, Miss MacPhail? I don't think I've seen you without them before."

"Broken and not to be fixed until Wednesday."

"Well, I hope you get them back in good stead. I rather like the owlish look."

We entered the classroom together, and Mr. Chamberlain arranged stacks of paper on the table while I claimed my usual front row seat. I listened to his lecture on Tennyson, enthralled beyond reality, dutifully taking notes, then filled out my calendar with the proposed deadlines for papers, tests and readings, squinting at the page as I wrote. When class was over, I rose and moved toward the door, taking my time in case—yes! He called my name.

"Miss MacPhail!"

I floated over to his lectern, juggling my satchel of books, tucking stray hairs behind my ears. "Yes, sir?"

"Hold a moment. I want to walk out with you. There's something I want to talk to you about."

I felt faint. I couldn't speak beyond a weak, "Yes." My feet were like lead boots holding me to the floor, but my heart had already left my body and hovered above me.

Phillip Chamberlain took an interminable time gathering his notes and stuffing them into his leather brief case. He smiled and escorted me out of the room, down the stairs and out into the sunny September afternoon. I don't know to this day how I ever negotiated those stairs.

He walked along easily beside me, tall, dark and extremely fit for a college professor. I'd have been taken with him even if he weren't so handsome, but handsome dazzled my eyes. We passed other students and faculty as we walked, talking about, what else? Poetry. It was as though we two existed in our own cocoon, protected, intimate, alone.

"So you've written more poetry this summer, have you? I'd like to read it sometime. Your work is excellent, Miss MacPhail, truly Dickinsonian. What I wanted to ask you is this: I'm the faculty sponsor of the poetry magazine and I'd . . ."

"Poetry magazine? I didn't know there was a poetry magazine!"

"There hasn't been until now. It's just getting started, and I was wondering if you would be interested in editing it?"

"Edit? Why, Mr. Chamberlain, I don't know anything about editing. How could I be the judge of others' work? Thank you for the honor, but..."

"Nonsense, Miss MacPhail. You're over-qualified, my dear. You'd be a natural for the job."

I stopped and looked up at him. I knew those warm, brown eyes, that strong jaw, the one droopy eyebrow—had memorized every feature, every expression, every quirk since the first day I'd stepped into his classroom. He set down his briefcase and took me by the shoulders. "Come now, Miss MacPhail,—Sarah? May I call you Sarah? Consider it a favor to me. I need a competent editor, and you have all the skill to make this magazine a shining example."

Of course, I was thrilled beyond all reason. Being his editor meant being alone with him in closed door meetings, long evenings assembling the magazine, meeting deadlines, sharing our opinions of submissions. This was beyond anything I'd ever conjured in my dreams.

Within a week he'd secured a tiny office—no more than one end of a former cloak room in Founder's Hall—a typewriter, a desk with a lamp, and a supply of paper, pencils, envelopes and paper clips. We covered the wainscoted walls with pictures of poets, copied poems in longhand and pinned them up. For me, it was intoxicating, though I'd never drunk more than a glass of claret with dinner. I lived poetry for the entire term, to the neglect of my other studies. But who was to care? Mother was still getting over father's death, Andrew was gone to California, and little brother Ned was preoccupied with fishing and nothing else. So there was no one to slow me from falling over the abyss into love.

He became Phillip to me, and I Sarah to him. We worked well together, all very proper, with no physical expression, but I knew that he felt as I did, that this was a relationship for the ages.

As time passed, he shared his ambition—to go to New York and teach at Columbia University, climb to the chairmanship of the English Department, and spend the rest of his days writing poetry. Not at all modest of his talent, he promised me that he would one day be known as the greatest of the American poets and take his place alongside Bryant, Poe, Longfellow, even Emerson, as the epitome of American poetic tradition. Starry-eyed, I shared his dream, picturing myself at his side, warm in the glow.

Every year, a few weeks into the fall semester, Juniata College celebrated the new term with a tradition called Mountain Day. Without prior announcement, a Thursday was declared Mountain Day, all classes and school business cancelled. The whole student body, faculty and staff were transported out to Ardenheim, at the confluence of the Raystown and Juniata Rivers. In anticipation, upper classmen gathered a fleet of every kind of boat, and a veritable regatta took place at the meeting of the two rivers. Boats of every size and shape, bedecked with bunting, banners, flags and colors, skittered back and forth with the wind or floated gently with the current.

One boat in particular stood out for its colorful flags, flying in the brisk breeze, a neat little yellow pedal boat, propelled by human power—to the delight of all who watched. Piloted expertly by Bert Judge, it attracted all the young men, anxious to ply their skills and propel the little craft faster and farther than anyone else. The gaiety of the day transformed us from casual acquaintances to a close, tight-knit family. It was heady, indeed, for me, an unworldly maiden from Mt. Etna, to be included—nay, enmeshed—in such a sheltered and sheltering company.

As the afternoon shadows lengthened, people began to gather by the wagons for the trip back to Huntingdon, but Phillip asked me to go for a boat ride across to a jutting point of land with rivers on both sides.

"Walk with me to that bridge?" he asked, pointing to a rustic, covered bridge spanning the Raystown River about a quarter mile upstream from where we stood.

We meandered alone up the rust colored track along the river, lost in each other, until we stopped to look out the bridge windows into the water below. I picked up a pebble from the bridge floor and dropped it into the river, watching the ripples flow out.

I turned to him. "That will be the way of your poetry. The news of a great new poet will ripple out from here, ever wider, embracing the literary world, until Phillip Chamberlain will take his rightful place among the great."

He reached for me, and I yielded, pulled into his arms by a force I couldn't deny. His lips sought mine, found them, and clung. I passed from my own identity into his. I wanted nothing but to share his life, fill his every need, be his ministering spirit.

***

Little by little our lives entwined, always over the poetry magazine, always carefully guarded against any suspicion of an inappropriate relationship. Phillip lived in a single room in a house on Maple Avenue with a private entrance in the rear. One night, after we'd worked late on the magazine, he took my arm as we closed up the office, leading me around behind the building in the direction of his rooming house.

"Come on, let's walk. It's a beautiful night."

I went along willingly, daring to hope that we would share another kiss, another warm embrace. As we passed under a street lamp, Phillip reached into his pocket and handed me a folded piece of paper—a poem. I held it under the light to read as he stood before me, hands in his pockets, shoulders hunched against the crisp October night.

Were I but thine, my dear
Were I but thine tonight
My heart would know no fear
My love would hold the light
Oh, come with me, my darling
To where the waters flow
And let our hearts be full
And let our spirits grow
I'd show you wonders plenty
And love all burning bright
Were I but thine, my dear
Were I but thine tonight

Overcome with love, joy, passion, I rushed into his arms. He held me close, protecting me from all care, promising to love me and keep me in his heart forever. He took my hand and led me away from the light, kissed me again and again, then hurried me up the now dark street, around to the back door of his rooming house and into his room. He locked the door and carried me to his bed, fumbling with my clothes and his. I yielded, swept away by his passion, driven by the need to seal our mutual love.

Later, as I lay in Phillip's arms, still reeling from the weight of what I'd done, I noted the hour and rose hurriedly to find my things.

"Phillip! Darling, wake up! It's ten minutes to ten. I have to get back before Mrs. Wright locks the door."

He rolled over, sleepy, and reached for his trousers. I was already dressed, picking up my satchel when he groaned and fell back on the bed.

"You can make it on your own, can't you, love? I'm done for."

I rushed to him, kissed him, caressed his thick black hair. "Of course, darling. Of course."

I let myself out into the blackness, hurried around to the front of the house and down to Mrs. Wright's. She was standing in the entry way in her wrapper, keys in hand when I rushed up the steps.

"I'm sorry, Mrs. Wright—the poetry magazine. I lost track of time."

Giving me a skeptical nod, she locked the door behind me.

Upstairs, Claire was already asleep, so I undressed in the dark and crept into bed, my heart overflowing. What had just happened—what did it mean? As much to Phillip as to me? There in the darkness, full of joy tinged with apprehension, I fell asleep.

Back in our little cubby-hole office in Founder's Hall a few weeks later, I was typing some poems submitted by students, all the while hoping Phillip would stop by. Our love hadn't emerged from the shadows, but I found it more and more difficult to keep it hidden. Within the hour the door opened and my love entered. I rushed to him, then restrained myself, ever careful of showing affection even when we thought we were alone. Indeed, Phillip's job depended on it. Romantic relations with students were strictly forbidden. Everyone knew that.

Still, I moved close enough to touch his arm, and he reached for my hand and gave it a squeeze. "Is the layout done? I thought it might take a week or so, but you're so efficient, you've probably got it done already."

I smiled and lowered my eyes, pleased by the compliment.

He took off his heavy, wool coat and hung it on one of a row of iron hooks that gave weight to the theory that our 'office' had once been a cloak room. "I'm glad I asked you to edit for me. This thing would take up way too much of my time."

I smiled and picked up one of the poems from a student contributor, read it to myself and laid it aside. "Really. What makes these people think they're poets? Just because it rhymes doesn't mean it's poetry."

Phillip smiled. "Getting to be quite the critic, are you?" He moved to my side, glanced at the poem and pulled me into his arms, kissing my neck. "Come round tonight?"

"I can't, Phillip. I've got a big exam in botany tomorrow. I have to study."

"Indeed. Your diligence breaks my heart."

"Have you had dinner yet? Mrs. Wright serves at six, and she doesn't bear tardiness, but she does allow us to bring a guest to the table once a month."

"I would, but we don't want anyone to mistake our friendship for a romance, now, do we?"

"Oh, yes. You're right. Well, I've got to get on then. Mrs. Wright, you know." I rose and pulled my coat down from its hook. "Do you want to walk me back?"

"I think I'll stay here and try to wade through some of these submissions. I'll see you in class tomorrow." He stooped to give me a peck on the cheek.

Our romance continued through the fall, his room becoming our love nest, since his landlady's room was in the front of the house and the other boarders came and went that way. The private entrance made our comings and goings just that—private.

Phillip's ardor never waned when we were alone, but I began to feel a growing discontent with the way he treated me anywhere but in his room. There were times when he seemed to ignore me in public to a far greater extent than I felt necessary—as though his mind was some place else—like he wanted me to edit his magazine but not to make too much of our 'relationship.' I tried to shake off my doubts, but when they descended upon me in the dark of night, I trembled with fear that I'd allowed myself to be taken in—in this, the most intimate of relationships.

I left the office one cloudy December afternoon feeling not quite at ease, not quite content. I'd decided to break my silence and talk to Claire after dinner. I wouldn't necessarily tell her who, but I would reveal the cause of my beating heart. I felt so green at being in love; I needed some propping up.

All the boarders were assembled at the table, and, after greeting me, our talk turned to petty matters. Alice Mac Comber had a new coat that must have cost her father the price of a carriage. Did anyone notice the color of Betsy Cadwallader's hair these days? It certainly had a red tone to it, didn't it? Ruth Rotherman and Miles Cannaday were seeing a lot of each other since Mountain Day back in September. And did Lyddie Ambrose really think no one saw her go in the back door of Staley's Bar on Penn Street?

I waited patiently for the meal to be over, anxious to talk to Claire alone. Once upstairs, I opened the conversation. "I've been keeping a secret from you," I began.

"Really? What is it? Is it a man? Anyone I know?"

"No. You don't know him. He isn't from the college. He's—uh—from Huntingdon."

"What? A town boy? Really, Sarah, you should be careful. Everyone knows town boys are common."

"Not this one. This one is tall, handsome, smart and rich. Everything a girl dreams of." I added the 'rich' to throw her off.

"Well, aren't you going to tell me his name?"

"Not yet. But I do want to talk to you about how to proceed. I've never had a beau before."

"With caution. That's the only way to proceed with a town boy. With caution. Where'd you meet him, anyway? You barely ever leave campus."

"Uh, at home. Last year. His father's a preacher, and the son came along when he preached my father's funeral."

"That was fortuitous."

"Yes, well, we'd met before—at my Aunt Alyssa's house. He's enrolled at Susquehanna University in the theology department. He's going into the ministry, like his father."

I felt myself sinking deeper into my fabricated story, moving away from my purpose. Still, I wanted Claire to be my advocate, hoping she'd lend some expertise on dealing with Phillip.

"The ministry? Hmm. Not sure I'd want to be a preacher's wife. Too many busy bodies watching all the time. Anyway, what about him?"

"Well, I don't know. He seems . . . distant sometimes."

Now Claire jumped on my story. "Distant? How so? Does he write to you? Make plans for Thanksgiving break? Are you sure you're telling me everything? Come on, Sarah, fess up. Something's bothering you and I don't for one minute believe it's some town boy from Huntingdon."

"Oh, Claire, I didn't want to tell anyone. You have to swear to secrecy. Please."

"Okay, I swear. Does this by any chance have anything to do with Professor Chamberlain?"

I stopped in my tracks. "How do you know that?"

"Really, Sarah! Doesn't everyone? You spend every spare moment at the poetry magazine; you two have your heads together at every turn. You're starry eyed when he walks into a room, and you talk about little else but the poetry magazine."

I winced at my own folly. I always thought I could keep a secret, but apparently I'd deluded only myself. "Do you think anyone else suspects?"

"Of course they do. It's all they talk about when you're not around. That and the fact that Professor Chamberlain probably won't be here by the end of the term. It's only a matter of time until someone alerts the president to your little liaison."

"Oh dear. I'd no idea. Claire, this is worse than I thought. I hope no one has spoken to the Dean. Poor Phillip."

"Poor Phillip? He's a grown man and he knows the rules. He should have known you'd fall in love with him if he made you his editor. Anyone with any sense would know you were taken with him and that it would lead you out of bounds. Now you're both on the verge of disgrace. I wonder that you didn't confide in me sooner."

Chapter 5

Richard, 1902

Mrs. MacPhail sent word that I was to go pick up Sarah at Juniata on the twenty-first for her Christmas break. Excited to see her, I wore a pair of new wool trousers and a white cotton shirt under my mackinaw. Brushed my hair and wet it to get it to lie down, even though I knew it would freeze before I got to Fox Hollow. I got up early, hitched the horse to the little shay and set out for Huntingdon. Lord, it was cold. I'd brought a buffalo robe to cover us up with, but I wasn't sure it would be enough. We might have to warm up bricks in Mrs. Wright's oven to put under our feet.

I drove up to Mrs. Wright's house, covered the horse with a blanket, and mounted the front steps. Sarah was already waiting in the parlor, her cape, bonnet and muff on the chair. She seemed glad to see me, though distracted about something.

"You glad to be going home?" I asked.

"Yes, I guess so. I have final exams in January, so I'll have to study a lot."

"Hope you'll have time to skate. The ice on the canal is smooth as glass. We can have a fire and invite some of the neighbors. It'll be fun."

She nodded absently, not very excited about skating. That was disappointing. We'd always enjoyed skating on what was left of the canal every winter. Sarah was quite a good skater, while I was a clumsy oaf, but happy to make a fool of myself just to be near her.

By the time we got home we were both frozen, in spite of stopping to warm our bricks at the general store in Alexandria on the way. Sarah seemed in a hurry to get into the house when I dropped her off, so I took the shay around, unhitched the horse and wiped her down. Still freezing, I knocked on the kitchen door to get warm before the walk home. Mrs. Beck opened it with a cup of hot tea in hand to warm me.

"Where's Sarah?" I asked, hoping to get a few more minutes with her.

"Upstairs, I guess. She hasn't been out here yet." Mrs. Beck minded her own business, a trait appreciated in a household like the MacPhails.

I cast about for an excuse to linger in the warm kitchen on the outside chance that Sarah might wander in, but it was soon apparent that she would not. I took my leave and stepped out into the cold evening, buttoned my mackinaw, and made my way, head down, through the village. I lived in the little cottage across the track from the mill, where I'd grown up, as had the generations before me.

In those days, I thought often of getting married, but the only girl I'd ever wanted was probably spoken for by now, so I'd decided on a bachelor's life. I figured to keep the mill running as long as I could and then maybe look for other work. Out of loyalty and hope, I kept an eye on the MacPhail holdings up Roaring Run. No one asked me to, but I felt somehow that I should.

My house was almost as cold inside as out. I'd banked the fire, but it'd all but gone out, so I poked about among the ashes and located a few hot coals to use for a starter. The old chimney still had a strong draw, and it wasn't long before the fire was blazing. I sat down to a supper of cold mush left over from breakfast before retiring to my bed in the corner by the fireplace. I'd slept in the loft as a boy, but now I kept myself quite comfortable in the single downstairs room.

The next morning, after I'd watered the stock I trekked over to the manor house to offer my services for any Christmas preparations that might be afoot, looking for an excuse to put myself in Sarah's company. Every year we rambled about the woods in search of trailing pine that we used to drape the mantels of the fireplaces in every room. Mt. Etna manor stood out as the most beautiful Christmas house in the Juniata Valley, a sleigh ride destination, complete with caroling, hot chocolate, and bounteous trays of cookies and sweets.

Mrs. Beck greeted me at the door with the unexpected news that Mrs. MacPhail—Miss Anna, we called her—had taken ill, so there would be no Christmas preparations that day. I didn't see Sarah or Ned, just Mrs. Beck, so I wandered back home, disappointed.

Miss Anna remained ill for the whole two weeks while Sarah was home, casting a pall over any Christmas doings. I made sure there was plenty of wood for the stove and fireplaces in the manor house, for the cold clung to the hills and valleys like moss. There were a few visitors—Cousin Will Trethaway and Miss Bethany came down from Altoona—but it was nothing like the old days when friends and family came from miles around and the manor house glowed with Christmas cheer. On the second of

January, Ned came to my door to announce that I was needed to take Sarah back to college the next day.

"How's your mother, Ned?"

"Poorly." He stood in the doorway, shifting his weight from one foot to the other, a dance designed to ward off frozen feet.

"Any idea what's wrong?" I asked.

"Aunt Beth and Cousin Will came down yesterday. Said it might be something called Whipple's Disease." He nodded vigorously as though for emphasis.

Beth MacPhail and Will Trethaway shared a medical practice in Altoona. Beth was getting up in years, and Will carried most of the load, but the only woman doctor in Altoona still had a full compliment of patients, mostly women, and a reputation for accurate diagnosis.

"What's that, Whipple's Disease?"

"I don't know, but I sure wish Mama would get better."

"Sarah going back to Juniata? Even if your mother's sick?"

"She says she has to go back for her exams." Ned nodded again, clearly uncomfortable with his mother's illness.

"Would you like to ride along when I take her back?"

"Uh huh. I better be going. See you tomorrow." I smiled. Ned's departures were always abrupt. No niceties. Just, "see you tomorrow."

The next morning I hitched the horse to the shay and tucked the buffalo robe around the three of us, to set out for another cold ride to Huntingdon. I could tell Sarah wasn't herself. Something was bothering her that I took to be her mother's illness. When we dropped her off at Mrs. Wright's, she hopped down and entered the house without even inviting us in to get warm.

"What do you make of that?" I asked Ned.

"Sarah has to study," he replied, tucking the robe tight around his butt.

Sarah

I didn't want to admit it, but my reason for hurrying back to college even though Mother lay ill, was my insecurity over Phillip. He'd seemed distant before I left, and didn't make any effort to keep in touch over the holidays—not even a Christmas greeting. I felt an almost desperate need to be back at school where I hoped my fears would somehow be abated. But my return brought anything but satisfaction. In the frenzy of studying for final exams, I saw little of Phillip, as my dreams for a life as the consort of the great American poet slowly melted away.

I feared Phillip was having second thoughts about indulging in a love affair with a student, and it was soon apparent that his position and his future career meant more to him than I did. Worried, I told him about my conversation with Claire.

"You told her what?"

"Nothing, really. Just that we cared for each other, and . . ."

"My God, Sarah, surely not! Surely you didn't let Claire think we were lovers."

"Not lovers, really. I just said . . ."

"And she said everyone knew? Knew what, for God's sake?" He became suddenly agitated—crumpled up a poem he was reading, looked about the office, grabbed his coat and jerked the door open. He stalked away without another word, leaving me to agonize over my failings.

Within the week he was called into the president's office and interrogated for more than an hour about his private life. Afraid of being dismissed in disgrace, Phillip denied all—said it was a mistaken judgment based on our 'professional' relationship with the magazine. He was let off with a stern warning of immediate dismissal should any further gossip reach the president's ears.

I was working in the office when he came straight from the president with this announcement: "The poetry magazine is no longer sponsored or countenanced by the college."

Without looking at me, he began to pull things out of the desk and off the walls, in a great hurry to wipe his own—if not our—slate clean. I rose and watched as he obliterated every scrap of evidence of the magazine and of our love.

"I'm sorry, Phillip. I never meant to put your future in jeopardy. Please, we can bide our time until I graduate, or, better yet, I could just drop out of school."

He went on dumping items from the desk into a box, not responding to my pleas. When the box was loaded, he picked it up under one arm and the big, heavy typewriter under the other and looked to me to open the door.

I stepped in front of it. "Please tell me this doesn't mean . . ."

He stepped around me, hefting the typewriter in one arm and the box in the other. "You can do as you please, Sarah. I've no claim to you or your future. I must look to my own, as you must surely understand. I should have been wiser than to let this happen in the first place, and I can assure you, as I did the president, that there is no need for concern and there never was."

With that, he was gone. Out the door and away to wherever was the farthest he could get from me. Stunned, I looked around the bare room, now reverted back to coat hooks and wainscoting. How devastated. How empty. I picked up my coat and scarf and stepped out of the dark, empty hall into the bright, cold January sunlight.

I didn't know where to turn. If I went back to Mrs. Wright's, all the other boarders would know something had happened. I knew I couldn't bear to try to be normal in the face of devastation, so I walked down Moore Street to Second, then down to Penn Street and on to where Standing Stone Creek flowed into the Juniata River. There I sat down on a log overlooking the water and gave way to tears.

My brief sojourn into the world of romance had left me empty and humiliated. How could I have been so naïve? So completely trusting? No. Not completely. There'd always been that shadow of doubt hovering over me. My heart felt like a lead weight, pulling me down into an abyss.

I didn't want to see anyone, talk to anyone, be near any other human being. All I wanted was to go home, leave Juniata College and return to the place I knew best—Mt. Etna. There was no one to transport me and my things, and I couldn't bear to go back to pack them up. I'd go home on the train and send for my possessions later. So after about an hour, of crying, self-recrimination and regret, I wandered slowly back to the train depot near Fourth Street and purchased a ticket on the next train home.

It was after six when the train chugged to a stop at the Mt. Etna depot, a short walk from the manor house. I disembarked and started toward home in the winter twilight, flooded with anguish and regret, shivering—from the cold? Now my thoughts turned to the home I'd left so carelessly in my headlong drive to fulfill my longing for love. How could I have been so callous as to make light of my mother's illness? How could I have left her when she and Ned needed me so much? How could I even dream of leaving this place that had been my home and my family's home for generations? My fate was sealed. I willed all thoughts of Phillip Chamberlain out of my mind and let myself in the front door.

Before I could take off my scarf and coat, Ned was upon me. "Sarah! What are you doing home? Are you going to stay? I'll tell Mrs. Beck you're here."

Excited, he talked fast, running his words together.

"Yes, Ned, I'm home to stay. You can tell Mrs. Beck I'm here. I'll just run upstairs to freshen up for dinner."

At the top of the stairs, I turned left into my parents' bedroom, where my mother lay, wan and pale, her hands twitching nervously over the counterpane. I went to her bedside, saddened to find her even weaker than before, her face empty of vitality.

"No better, Mama?" I asked.

"No better, I'm afraid," she apologized. "What brings you home, dear?"

"Oh, nothing. I finished my exams, so I thought I'd come home to see how you were getting on," I lied.

"Not very well. I can't seem to throw this off. I get weaker every day."

My mother, only forty-seven, had always been so full of energy; it was shocking to see her lying abed. She'd taken my father's death hard but seemed to have gotten through her grief. Now this illness.

"I've decided to take the spring term off and stay here with you."

"Oh, dear, you shouldn't do that. I'll be all right soon. You go back to school."

"No, my mind is made up. I'll finish a little later, is all. What's important now is for you to get well."

Mother raised herself up on one elbow and beckoned me to her bedside. Bending down to receive her kiss, I felt a flood of relief, even peace, sure my decision was right.

"Mama," I began, tears forming in my eyes. "I've been foolish. So very foolish. I never should have left Mt. Etna."

She reached out and caressed my cheek with the back of her hand. "It's all right, dear. But you must promise me one thing."

"Anything, Mama."

"Take care of your brother for me. And Mt. Etna. For me and your father and all the ones who came before. Can you promise me that?"

"But Mama, you're going to get better. You'll be here doing all of that for years to come."

"No, Sarah. No. This isn't going to let go of me."

The tears fell unchecked now. I laid my head on her bed, my shoulders shaking with grief. "Yes, Mama. I promise. All that and more. I'll take care of Ned, and I'll never leave Mt. Etna. Never."

Downstairs in the parlor again, I stood looking out the front window at the old canal bed and the railroad track with the river beyond. This was all I'd ever known. Going to college didn't matter any more. Betrayed and alone, I let go of all that and cried until there were no more tears, then sent word to Richard Trethaway to go retrieve my belongings from Mrs. Wright's house.

Mother lingered until near the end of February but slipped away from us one dark night when the wind didn't blow and the cold seemed to penetrate the stone walls of the manor house. Ned and I sat at her bedside while Auntie Beth and Will ministered to her, but we knew she was leaving us and there was no way to stop her. Now I had even more reason to feel sorry for myself. Not only was I awash in unrequited love, but my mother had gone away and I had nothing left but the responsibility for the remains of Mt. Etna and a brother most people thought of, in their kindest way, as strange.

Chapter 6

Sarah, 1902

I spent the month of March in seclusion, refusing to see anybody or to respond to the notes and letters that came almost daily from Juniata College. Once spring arrived in April, I realized that whatever my emotional plight, I had an estate to manage—get repairs done, maintain the buildings, and rent out empty houses and cabins. The result of all of this, of course, was to provide a cushion against the deep disappointment and loneliness that lurked at the edge of my being.

Managing the estate seemed never-ending but, driven by a need to keep busy, I filled my days with work instead of dreams and regret. I didn't hear from Phillip, even though I still nursed a deep longing for him, secretly dreamed of seeing him get off the train at the depot and come striding and smiling to my arms.

When summer came I tried to get out more, went visiting in Williamsburg, and took Ned to Altoona for a few days. Cousin Will and Aunt Beth were always gracious about Ned. They saw him as unique and interesting, while I saw nothing but a lifelong obligation.

We had many a conversation about Ned—whether he would ever be able to get along on his own, whether he was some kind of crazy, or whether he was just different. Having lived with him since I was five, I was used to his solitary ways, the blank look he turned on anyone he didn't know; but I had my own hurts to nurse, and sometimes I wanted nothing more than to be free of him.

That summer we settled into a simple routine of household chores, gardening, canning and caring for the estate. I did, that is. Ned went fishing, cut new fishing poles, found new fishing holes, caught fish—but always threw them back. Ned was like that. He couldn't bear to hurt a living thing, and fishing was his greatest pleasure as long as the fish were returned to the stream unharmed. As for our mother's passing, that was one more puzzle about Ned. He never shed a tear, never said he missed her, never talked about her at all. It'd been that way with Papa, too, leading me to wonder if my brother was capable of feeling for anything but fish.

The only visitor I had that summer was unexpected. Bert Judge rode up on her sprightly little mare one cool morning as I was in the garden picking peas.

"Why, Bert! What a surprise to see you!"

"Yes, well, you left school so abruptly I thought maybe you needed a friend. Then I heard your mother died, and I knew you needed one."

Flattered by her offer of friendship, I smiled, pulled off my bonnet, and invited her to the porch for a glass of iced tea. "How did your spring semester go?" I asked.

"Okay. Could have been better. Papa always gets apoplectic when my grade sheets come in. They came yesterday, so I thought I needed to be gone somewhere today." She slapped her riding crop smartly against her woolen riding pants, then asked, abruptly, "Where did your brother Andrew go?"

"To California. For six years—maybe more."

"Could I have his address? I'd like to write to him."

The prospect of any kind of friendship between Bert Judge and Andrew wasn't pleasing. I still had hopes for Andrew and Claire to get together and, in any case, Bert didn't pass muster as sister-in-law material. Too modern. But there was no polite way to deny her request, so I wrote down Andrew's address and gave it to her.

It seemed that, having gotten what she came for, Bert felt no further need for my company, for she was up and mounted and riding away before the ink had dried, stopping at the mill to chat with Richard on her way past.

1903

Since I'd ignored their efforts to keep up with me, I'd fallen out of touch with my Juniata College friends as they finished their junior year, giddily looking forward to graduation the next June. Inevitably, I felt left out of things and limited my correspondence to Claire, who wrote me weekly, hinting broadly that she would love a weekend in the country if I were inclined to extend an invitation.

Still embarrassed by my humiliation, I put her off, not sure I wanted to nurture our friendship. I let that first summer go by without issuing the invitation. Summer passed into fall and winter, and by spring, as those old college relationships had started to fade, there came an invitation from Claire to attend graduation in June. I'd no desire to witness that milestone as a spectator, so I sent my regrets. Not to be put off, Claire invited herself for a visit two weeks later, and I relented, hoping enough time had passed that my shame might have faded into oblivion.

Claire looked around at the run-down little village and the big, imposing manor house, looking somewhat worn around the edges, and remarked, "You certainly have your hands full here. Really, Sarah, you should have stayed and finished your studies at Juniata. Whatever will you do with yourself in this place?"

"Oh, Mt. Etna can be exciting in its own way."

Claire shook her head and winced. "Who are you trying to convince? Me or you?"

I looked away. So she saw my home and way of life as quaint, old fashioned, out of style. Quite haughty of her, considering her own origins. I tried to assure her that this place was significant for its history alone, but she wasn't listening.

"Anyway, I came because I have some news that won't wait. It's still a secret, but I wanted to tell you because I know it will be a shock and I didn't want it to affect our friendship."

"Really, Claire? What is it?"

"Well . . ." She hesitated, looking ill at ease. "I didn't want you to hear this from anyone else. I've been seeing Phillip Chamberlain—on the sly, you see—and he's asked me to marry him."

Dumb silence followed her revelation. I didn't know whether I was hurt, angry—or both. It seemed so deceitful, so mean, I couldn't absorb it.

"Now, Sarah, please don't be angry. You know as well as I do these things happen—not by choice, but by chance. I certainly never set out to fall in love with Phillip, it just happened."

She took a handkerchief from her waistband and dabbed her eyes. "You're hurt, my dear. Oh, I'm so sorry. You were on my mind the whole time. I tried not to fall in love, but I felt so sorry for him, with the trouble over you and fearing he might lose his job."

"So he was willing to take the risk of losing his job with you, but not with me? And you, knowing how I felt, rushed into his arms as though I didn't exist? Had never existed? How could you, Claire?"

I knew I should be gracious, wish them well with superficial politeness, but the truth was, I wanted to slap her, pull her hair, rip her clothes. Instead, I stood there in the middle of the parlor, hands at my sides, gazing over Claire's head as though I'd never seen the room before. The settee, the chairs, the drapes at the windows—all as though I hadn't spent my whole life there. As though I'd just walked into the room for the first time. Every picture, every ripple in the window glass, the brocade chair and velvet settee, all appeared new and unfamiliar.

"I think you'd better go, Claire. Take the next train back to Lewistown and don't come back. And please don't invite me to your wedding or expect me to share your joy." My voice came out strong and measured, not at all distraught, though I was.

Reproached and reduced to real tears, she whispered, "There is no train until tomorrow. I'm bound to spend the night. Really, Sarah, I'd hoped you'd accept this with grace. You could have found out from others, but I wanted to spare you the embarrassment of running into someone from school and finding out by the gossip grapevine."

"Thank you so much for the consideration."

"Now, Sarah, don't burn your bridges," she entreated. "Life can take some varied turns. You never know when you might need a friend."

"Need you? Why would I ever need someone like you—someone who's watched my humiliation and then stepped up to gather the spoils? Take your things to the servants' quarters over the kitchen. I don't ever want to see you again."

With that, she left the room. I waited until I couldn't hear her footsteps in the room above, then ascended the stairs myself and fell onto my bed in tears. Claire and Phillip? How could they? Why didn't they just move far away and never let me know? Why was this being hurled in my face?

I didn't go down to dinner. When Mrs. Beck came up to ask why I was absent, I made up an illness and sent my apologies to Claire. Let her sit there with Ned and listen to his interminable talk about fish until she wanted to scream. I would stay in seclusion, and she could rot in hell.

Chapter 7

Richard, 1903

One afternoon that summer, Ned came running up the track to Roaring Run Hollow full of excitement. "Richard, you should see! They're building that new town down the river—a real town!"

"A town? Really? Where will they get people to fill it?"

"It's a workers' town. I heard the builder talking about it to one of the carpenters. They're building a whole lot of houses for the quarry workers to live in."

Well, things were alive again around Mt. Etna. I wished they'd rent some of the MacPhail's old buildings to house their workers, but it seemed the stone company was intent upon building a company town with a company store, a school and about thirty houses. The houses went up quickly, and workers with families to fill them followed. At first, the workers were local people, glad for employment, since the iron industry had gone away, but it wasn't long before strange, new people arrived—swarthy, dark people who didn't speak English and whose names were impossible to pronounce.

"Why are they bringing these people in here to work? Don't we have enough local people to fill those jobs?" Sarah quizzed me one day when I stopped by with a bushel of apples I'd picked off the tree behind the mill.

"Quarryin' is hard work. Not that farmin' isn't, but they don't pay much, and these foreigners are willing to work for practically nothing. They get their house and a garden spot, small wages, and a company store where they can spend all they earn and go into bond for the rest."

"Well, they can bring these foreigners in, but how do they expect them to be like us? They'll always be different. I don't feel comfortable with all these new people mucking about."

"Whoa there, Sarah. That's the same thing folks said about the Germans or the Irish or anybody else that came after they did. We were all foreigners once."

"Well," she sniffed. "This is different. At least they spoke English."

"Not all of them, but it didn't take them long to learn. These people will learn, too." I smiled. Knowing Sarah, she'd resist for as long as it took her to get to know some of these people, and then everything would be all right.

To Sarah's dismay, Ned was enthralled by all the excitement at Blair Four. He spent day after day watching them build the town. The quarrying went on as the construction continued, and freight trains stopped daily at Blair Four to load the cars with tons of limestone rock destined for the steel mills.

Ned watched all this from the tall branches of an oak tree he'd climbed near the building site, keeping himself well hidden among the branches and moving from that tree to another when the crews started a new house. He never spoke to anyone or bothered them, but they had to know he was there all the time—watching.

I took it as my duty to keep an eye on him and steer him clear of trouble. These new people didn't know him, weren't aware of his foibles, and would laugh at him at best and do him violence at worst. So I tried to keep an eye on his movements. Sarah was even more concerned than I was, setting up boundaries for him closer to the house and enjoining him not to go to Blair Four unless I or one of our other neighbors went with him.

It didn't work. Ned chafed under any restraint of his movements and resented being treated like a child, even though that's exactly what he was—in Sarah's eyes, at least. So he would sneak off to Blair Four whenever her back was turned and come home by way of my house, full of stories about the progress of operations there.

Sarah decided it was time to find some way to keep Ned busy and out from under the influence of people who might lead him astray. She enlisted the help of some of the neighbor boys to play ball with him or go fishing to distract him from what had become an obsession.

She worried that Ned, socially inept at best, would wander into trouble with a rough lot and bring disaster upon himself. She even threatened to chain him to a tree—not that she would, of course, but desperation clouds the mind.

Sarah and I had many a discussion over Ned's desire for freedom and her fears for his safety. I argued that he just wanted to be a man with all the freedoms and habits that connoted, but Sarah couldn't just let him follow his whims. God knew where that might lead, so she tightened her rules and spent way too much time watching him, preventing him, lecturing him until we were all exhausted with it.

Then, one afternoon, I was sweeping out the mill when Sarah came tripping down the track, exasperation flowing from her pores.

"Richard, you've got to help me. I was weeding my flower bed when I realized that Ned was gone—sneaked off to Blair Four . . . *again!*" She sat down on a bench outside the mill and wiped her brow with a corner of her apron. She looked at me, pleading. "Please, Richard. I don't know what to do with him."

"I'll go see if I can find him," I said. Leaving her seated on the bench, I proceeded down the track toward Blair Four. As I wandered up and down the two well-ordered streets, I couldn't help but be impressed with the neat little houses with lilac bushes and fruit trees in the dooryards. It was a much nicer place than I'd expected. A dark looking woman, hardly more than a girl, really, hair tied up in a scarf, was hanging her laundry on a line strung from her house to a tree.

"Pardon me, but have you seen a young man with curly blond hair—about this tall—around here?" I gestured in the air with my hand above my head. Ned was a strapping youth, outdid me by three or four inches.

She gave me a blank stare, looked around for someone to rescue her, and shook her head. "No Engli," she said. "No Engli." She pointed behind me to a large building with concrete steps leading to a wide front door. "Store."

"Oh, thank you. I'll ask there."

The store was run by the company, and therefore had an English speaking clerk and manager. Hesitant to call attention to Ned, lest they think him odd, or worse, I entered and looked about as though shopping. Everything was on high shelves behind the long wooden counter, in locked barrels or kegs, or hanging high, out of reach. The clerk used a stick—like a long broom handle with a hook on the end—to pull items from the top shelves and catch them as they fell. I waited as he served another customer, hoping to speak with him alone to minimize attention to Ned.

As I looked around, trying to think of how to ask, I turned and saw Ned ambling down the street—just a wagon track, really—as though he were quite at home. I turned and ran from the store, calling him.

Ned saw me and stopped, hands in his pockets, cap askew.

"Richard! Whatcha doin' here? Hey, wanna go fishin' this afternoon?"

"Your sister's worried about you. She sent me over here to fetch you back."

"Oh, I know. She's always fussin' over me. I'm fine. I can take care of myself."

I reached out and gently placed my hand on the back of his neck, like a collar. "She's just concerned for you. She means well."

"I don't care. She ain't my mother. I can do on my own." Then he pulled away, strode out in front of me and started to run.

"All right, Ned. Wait up. We need to talk."

Never slackening his pace, he tore down along the railroad, kicking up cinders in globs. I knew I'd never catch him, so I slowed to a walk and followed him back toward the manor house. I entered by the kitchen door, calling his name.

"He ain't here," Mrs. Beck looked at me with raised eyebrows, wiping her floury hands on her apron. "Begging your pardon,

Richard, but Miss ain't going to be able to control him for long. He's big enough and sly enough to get around her any way he wants. She's got her hands full with that one."

I sighed and sank down onto a straight-backed kitchen chair. "I know, but she's going to have to let him have his head or he'll do something really dumb, like run off."

"She should just let him go. He'll be all right. Knows his way around, and folks here are used to him."

"Here maybe, but he won't stay away from Blair Four. Those people over there *don't* know him. Ned does dumb things sometimes, and they might take him the wrong way, like an insult or something. I don't want him to get hurt."

"Well, it ain't my place to be saying, but maybe Miss'll just have to let him find his own way. You know. Take his punishment when he slips up and he'll learn better."

She filled the tea kettle and set it on the stove. The kitchen had been modernized some. There was an ice box in the corner that I kept supplied with ice cut from the canal sloughs in the winter and stored in the spring house. They still used kerosene lamps, but Will and Beth were encouraging Sarah to get electricity, and they insisted on having a telephone installed so they could keep in touch when the need arose. It kept me busy cutting and stacking firewood, cutting and storing ice and looking after the horses. I'd never say anything, of course, but I don't know where they'd been without me, that big house and all.

As I sat drinking my tea, looking out the window, I saw Ned walking back through the village, hands in his pockets, cap askew, as usual. My heart went out to him. He looked like any other handsome young man out for a stroll, but his head was someplace else, not where most peoples' was. As I watched, a man on horseback rode up beside him. The man tipped his hat and said something to Ned, who reared back as though afraid, looked around in panic and made a right turn into the garden patch.

That's right, brother of mine. Watch out for strangers. Don't talk to them or look at them. They might be dangerous.

Chapter 8

Will Trethaway, 1904

I knew as soon as the phone rang it was Ned. Just knew, in my gut. I hadn't heard from my young cousin in a couple of months, so I was due.

"Hello?"

"Will? Can you come down? I need to talk."

"Sure, Ned. I'll be down on Sunday. That soon enough?"

"I guess so. I really need to talk."

"What do you want to talk about?"

"Her."

"Sarah? That her?"

"Yeah. She's on me all the time. Won't leave me alone. I'm gonna run away."

Ned, nineteen, socially awkward, withdrawn, not quite together, talked about running away on a regular basis. "Where would you run to, Ned?"

"I don't know. I'd just run. She won't leave me alone."

The extent of Sarah's interference with Ned's life was to monitor his comings and goings and put up unenforceable rules about just about everything. I can't say I blamed him for wanting to run away, but there was the question of how well he'd get along away from the shelter of the manor house at Mt. Etna. Ned was different. Sarah insisted he was slow, but I never thought that. He was bright enough and very perceptive, but she'd made it her purpose in life to take care of her "unfortunate" brother, so she could easily make a case for his being slow.

Ned didn't get everything there was to get, mostly about people. In the company of strangers he'd start looking for a quick escape and, lacking that, he'd get distraught. In the worst of conditions, he'd sit in a corner and rock back and forth, keening to himself.

So I couldn't really blame Sarah for trying to protect him, but protect isn't that far from control, and Ned knew it. Even though he'd never had a real conversation with anyone but family, Ned was convinced he was capable of making it on his own. My thought was to ease him into a wider social life—let him come stay in Altoona with Beth and me. Let him find his way in the world at his own pace. Maybe, with a little patience and encouragement, he'd turn out just fine.

"Tell you what, Ned. I'll be down Sunday and I'll talk to her. Help her see your side of things. That okay?"

"Uh-huh. I guess so."

I could tell by the flatness in his voice that it wasn't really okay. But a surgeon with a serious practice can't just pick up and leave any time the phone rings. "Okay, then. See you Sunday."

"Right, Will. Sunday."

I felt badly about leaving him hanging like that, but I really had no choice. His sister, five years Ned's senior, had made a project of him since their mother died, so it would be a tussle to gain any kind of freedom for him.

The door to the inner office opened and Aunt Beth emerged, her energy level belying her seventy plus years. "Who was on the phone?"

"Ned."

"Running away again?"

I nodded. "Wants me to come down on Sunday and rescue him from Sarah's clutches."

Beth's blue eyes twinkled behind her wire rimmed glasses. "I'm for Ned. Sarah makes too much of everything these days."

"Yes, but I feel for her, too. Something must have happened at Juniata that turned her in on herself and away from the world. If she didn't have Ned to dote on, she'd become a recluse."

"Or, if she didn't have Ned to control, she just might find something else to do."

"Maybe. Anyway, come down there with me. I'll need fortification. Sarah can be a formidable woman when she wants to be, and she wants to be most of the time."

Beth laughed.

At noon on Sunday we alighted from the cars at the Mt. Etna depot. I still found it amazing that we could catch a train in Altoona and be in Mt. Etna in about an hour with stops in Hollidaysburg, Frankstown, Canoe Creek and Williamsburg. I took Beth's arm and carried the hamper she'd brought along filled with city food—things the little Mt. Etna store didn't carry. We walked up the cinder track to the bridge over the old canal basin, empty now and sprouting trees and grass.

The manor house looked the same as always. Sarah wasn't one for change, and her father, my Uncle Laird, had been a stickler for keeping to the old ways. His widow, Anna, had tried to redecorate after he died, but Sarah had been deliberate in turning everything back once Anna was gone, too.

Ned had seen the train coming and watched our progress from the porch. He didn't hail us or run to meet us, but stood tall, arms crossed, cap askew, blond hair jutting out at every angle. Handsome lad, whatever was going on in his head.

"Hey, Will, Auntie. I've been waiting for you."

"Ned, old boy, what is it this time?" I asked.

"Same old stuff. She says I have to stay close, just around here. Says she doesn't want me hanging around those foreigners over at Blair Four, and I ain't allowed to smoke, cuss, drink beer or play cards. It's what men *do,* Will. Why can't she understand I'm a man?"

I shook my head and closed my eyes to keep from smiling. Same old stuff indeed.

Beth carried the hamper right through the center hall to the table in the middle of the kitchen. Mrs. Beck unloaded the food and arranged it on her pantry shelves.

Sarah was waiting for us in the parlor, sitting prim, her feet resting on a neat little footstool, stitchery in her lap.

"I suppose he's been on the telephone, fussing about every little thing."

She didn't give me time to lean down a give her a kiss on her soft, young cheek. At twenty-four, she was still quite attractive, but I feared well on her way to drying up, ever since what I guessed was an ill-advised love affair and whatever disaster had followed. I suspected that her riveted focus on Ned stemmed from that.

"Well, my dear, it seems you've got his dander up this time. He's adamant about running away."

"Let him," she sniffed. "Take him home with you. You'll soon see what I have to put up with. It won't take him twenty-four hours to find out he can't get on by himself and come running home to hide behind my skirts."

"Quite probably. Maybe we should just let him try."

Sarah put down her stitchery, clearly irritated. "I don't think he's up to it, but I guess we can let him try. He's not prepared for the realities of life, Will. He'll get into trouble and bring disgrace on himself and us, sure enough."

"You seem so sure he couldn't make it on his own, but I don't know. He just might surprise you. Anyway, we'll never know unless we give him a chance."

She jammed the stitchery into her bag and rose from the velvet settee. "William Trethaway, you don't have to put up with his bellyaching or worry where he is and what's happening to him day after day. I do, and I know what I'm talking about. He's never even made a friend. Spent his childhood fishing. You'd think fish were interesting or something, the way he goes on about them. A fish is a fish. That's all."

Ned stood in the doorway, arms crossed, listening to his sister's tirade. Sarah brimmed with authority. She might be forty years younger than I was, but her steely determination intimidated even me. In spite of my intention to find some compromise to give Ned more freedom, I felt my resolve begin to wilt under Sarah's barrage.

"Well, then. Ned, let's go in the kitchen and see what Mrs. Beck is getting up for dinner."

Ned followed me, meek and mild, until we closed the parlor door. "See what I mean, Will? She just wants to control me all the time. I gotta get away. Can I come live with you and Auntie Beth?"

"You could come live with me, I guess—for a while, at least. Auntie Beth has Uncle Harrison to look after, remember? He's not been well these past few years."

Beth really could have and perhaps should have retired by now, but, like her young niece, Beth was a woman of purpose. Fortunately, her purpose had always been healing the sick, so she tended not to meddle. She did admonish me for letting Sarah "run all over me" and for agreeing to let Ned "run away" to my house.

I knew she was right, but I saw Ned in a different light. I was sure he'd get along fine, given the chance, and I wanted very much to give him that chance.

Before we left Mt. Etna I always made it my business to stop by and see Tess Gorman, in whose shadow I'd grown up. Tess was the child of Phoebe Baker and Lem Trethaway, a pair of star-crossed lovers whose offspring had grown up in the shelter of her Grandmother Lindy's careful tutelage. Six years younger, I was the product of another ill-fated love affair, so I always thought Tess and I understood each other.

This Sunday afternoon, Tess was sitting out under a huge sycamore that shaded the little house where my Grandma Ellie used to live, smoking a corn cob pipe and swatting flies with a rolled up newspaper.

"Good day, Cousin Tess. How goes life with you?"

"Who's that? Will?" It was one more indicator that her eyesight was failing.

"Yes. It's me."

"What brings you here? Sarah and Ned feudin'?"

She peered at me, frowning.

"No need to tell you, Tess. You don't miss a thing."

"A mite now and then. Can't see worth a damn, and my hearin's going right along with my eyes. Hell, gettin' old."

"Come to Altoona and I'll get you fixed up with a pair of glasses. Good as new in a half hour." I'd tried to get her to wear glasses before, but she was adamant that glasses were for vanity and no other purpose.

"Will Trethaway, you think you can fix about anything. Bushwah. You can't fix old."

"Maybe I can't, but I can smooth the path."

She puffed on her pipe and humphed. "What you doin' down from Altoona, is what I want to know."

"Same old trouble. Ned wants to grow up and be a man, and Sarah wants to prevent him. What do you think I should do?"

"Butt out and let him do what he will. He ain't a danger to nobody. Just let him grow to manhood. Tell Sarah that."

"Think I'll take him to Altoona for a while. Give him a chance to broaden his horizons."

"Went there myself long time ago. It's good to fly the nest; even if you come back, you learn."

"So you approve of letting him try his wings, do you?"

"I approve of letting folks live their own lives. That's what I approve of. Tell Sarah that."

So, with the hamper reloaded with Mrs. Beck's pickles, preserves, canned peaches and canned tomatoes, we sat at the depot waiting for the evening train, Ned beside me, his carpet valise by his feet, cap still askew, looking off down the tracks.

"It's time for the 6:45. It's always three minutes late. Gets slowed down on the grade from Huntingdon, but makes it up along the river to Williamsburg."

I nodded. Ever since he was a wisp of a boy Ned had made a study of two things: fish and trains. Fish claimed his primary interest, but he found trains fascinating, knew every locomotive and how much it could pull, memorized time tables and schedules.

"Can I have my own room at your house, Will?"

"Sure, Ned. You know my house is way too big for just me. You can have all the room you want."

"I'm gonna get a job, too. At the Green Avenue Market, selling chickens and vegetables."

"Oh? That's what you think you'll do?"

"Yeah. Every Saturday. Then I'll have my own money that I can spend any way I want. Can I buy a cigar to smoke at your house?"

"I can't say I'd mind that, if you bought me one, too. How'd that be?"

"That'd be swell, Will. We can be best friends."

Sitting beside us listening to the conversation, Beth smiled. She knew all of Sarah's rules about smoking, swearing, drinking beer and playing cards would be tested and stretched to the breaking point at my house, and she was looking forward to it.

As the train puffed around the bend from Huntingdon, the evening shadows cast a soft, gray light along the river. I glanced over at Ned, sitting tall, alive with anticipation. Nice boy. Always had been. It should be all right for a nice kid to be a little strange.

Chapter 9

Will, 1904

I must admit, I was a little apprehensive about Ned getting a job at the Green Avenue Market. He'd never really been tested in the wider world, and I wondered how he'd take to having to talk to strangers on a regular basis. I decided not to push him, but to stay in the background and support him if needed. Needed came along pretty quick.

That first morning, after breakfast, Ned put on his cap and stood looking at me as though I were keeping him from some errand.

"What are you going to do today, Ned?"

"Well, *you* know. I'm going to get a job. At the Market. I told you."

"Well, Ned, the market is only open on the weekends—Friday afternoon and Saturday all day. If you want to work there, you'll have to wait until Friday about noon and go looking then."

"Oh. Well, what am I going to do now? I want something to do. Can I go down and look at the shops?"

Altoona's railroad shops were the largest and busiest in the entire country. Practically every man in town worked for the Pennsylvania Railroad in some capacity, and Ned found some way to get a first-hand view of the shops every time he came to town, to the amazement of his Aunt Beth and me. He'd go out early and come home late, dirty and happy, as though he'd been to a circus or some magic show—full of talk about trains. Once, he'd somehow gotten into the painting shop where they painted the stripes on the cars, and he came home full of admiration for his 'friends', the stripers.

So when he asked to go to the shops, I assumed he meant to walk along the fence and look in—or maybe take up station on one of the foot bridges that spanned the tracks—and watch the continuous coming and going around the switch yard.

Beth and I were preoccupied with our medical practice, so when Ned left we turned to our work and didn't give him another thought until Miss Powell, our nursing assistant, entered the dispensary to tell us that there was a police officer outside with Ned in tow. Beth was occupied with sewing up a workman's severely cut hand, so I was charged with seeing what the policeman could want.

"Good day, officer. What can I do for you?"

The policeman, disgruntled, shoved a disheveled Ned toward me. "Keep this young fool out of the rail yard, for one thing. Like to get his dumb ass killed hanging around there. Stepped right in front of a switcher this morning. Then when I yelled at him, he run off. Could have been the end of him. You know, Doc, boys like him need watching better. Seems a little tetched in the head. Get himself knocked off, like as not, one of these days."

I winced as the man went on about how dumb and foolish Ned was and how I should be more supervisory if I was to be his guardian. I watched Ned's face as the man said the words dumb, stupid and tetched so many times I wanted to thrash him.

"Okay, officer. I get it. I'll keep better track of him. Thank you for bringing him home."

"Ye'd be thankin' me for bringing his dead carcass home if I hadn't been there to see his antics this mornin'."

"Yes, yes. You said that. Now I'll take care of him."

The policeman slapped his night stick against his palm. "Ye'd better. I catch him down by the shops again, I ain't makin' no promises. Might just *let* him get hisself killed. Damn loony."

Normally restrained, I felt myself let go. "All right! You've said enough. You've no idea what you're talking about. He probably knows more about trains than you do, so thank you—and be gone!"

The man reared back as though I'd taken a swing at him. "Why, you insolent bastard! I'm just doing my job. You keep that nut away from the rail yard. Hear?"

I grabbed Ned's arm and practically stuffed him in the side door of the house. The policeman humphed and turned toward the street, yelling over his shoulder, "I shouldn't wonder if he ended up out at Hollidaysburg or worse!"

Hollidaysburg was the state hospital for the insane. I turned as though to follow him, but it was Ned's turn to restrain me. "It's okay, Will. He didn't mean anything by it."

But we both knew better. Ned wasn't stupid, loony, tetched or insane. But he wasn't like other young men—at least not on a social level. His lack of social acumen left him to the judgment of others less able than he but more ready to judge. I led him up the side stairs into the dispensary, where Miss Powell took one look at him and said, "Where'd you get that mouse under your eye? Stand too close to the track with the cinders a-flying?"

I frowned at Ned. "What's this?"

"Nothing. Just some kids. Thought they was having fun is all. They didn't mean nothing by it."

I turned him to face me. "You can't go around saying people don't mean anything by their actions. They do. They mean they think you're fair game to make fun of and harass. Did one of them hit you? Is that how you got a black eye?"

Ned nodded. "I just wanted to be their friend."

"Okay, Ned. We have to have a talk. A long talk. You can't go around trespassing on the railroad's property, and you can't just walk up to a group of young men you never saw before and expect them to embrace you as one of their own."

Ned sat down on a straight chair, took off his cap, and ran his fingers through his curls. "I don't get it, Will. I don't understand the rules. Everyone else but me does. I just wanted to see the trains up close. I wasn't going to hurt anything. And those boys, they were playing baseball. I wanted to play, too, but they just laughed and made fun of me. Why, Will?"

"I don't know, Ned. Maybe you said the wrong thing. Did the wrong thing. I wasn't there, or I'd tell you what it was. But maybe we need some lessons about making friends—getting on in the world. You can't go around getting in trouble all the time. You'll get a reputation for being queer, odd. You know, not right in the head."

Ned sighed. I guess I'm not, 'cause I don't know what to do or say, and I always get things wrong. Maybe Sarah's right."

Not for the first time, I thought she might be. Here we were, not twenty-four hours into my project for expanding Ned's social skills, and already in deep water. "Tell you what. I'll clear my schedule and you and I can go to the ball game at the Cricket Field this afternoon. How'd that be?"

"That'd be good, Will."

"Okay. Put your cap back on. We can stop at the bakery for a roll and maybe see if Mr. Paulini has any cooked sausages at the butcher shop. Put them together for a lunch."

We went off to the Cricket Field, across Chestnut Avenue from the railroad shops, munching our homemade sandwiches and studying the playbills plastered on the outside fence, touting the prowess of the Pennsy team's lineup, their schedule, and their record of five wins with only one loss so far that season. Ned kept looking over at the shop yards, but I put a restraining hand on his arm and guided him in through the gate.

It was a warm afternoon, and the Pennsy team had one heck of a pitcher, so the time dragged for Ned. He liked to see lots of hits, home runs, stolen bases. Instead, we got a no-hitter, which in itself should have been an experience. But Ned, being Ned, saw nothing to recommend a game where there wasn't even a single from the opposition and only an occasional hit for the home team. Pennsy won 1–0, not enough to placate Ned. My effort to smooth over the morning's events did little to salve his feelings or to distract him from the meanness of it.

We walked home in the lengthening shadows, Ned shuffling along beside me, deep in thought. "I hate being dumb," he mumbled.

"You're not dumb, Ned. Don't let that policeman get to you. He doesn't know who you are or anything about you. I do, and I say you're very smart. You just have trouble reading people."

"Well, I wish I didn't. I never get to do anything like other guys do. I can't go to parties or dances or shows. I don't ever get to have a girlfriend."

"Oh-ho! So that's what's on your mind! Girls. Why didn't you tell me? I could help with that!"

"Could you? Really? How?"

"Oh, I don't know. Maybe Auntie Beth could give a little party and introduce you to the daughters or granddaughters of some of her friends. That's easily done."

I don't know why I said that. I was entirely afraid that it would end in disaster, but I carried right through with the idea as though it were reasonable to think that Ned could navigate the terrors of female society unharmed. And I wasn't the only one. Beth seemed to think it worthwhile when I told her, and she went right ahead with the arrangements. So, on the following Saturday evening, a company of five girls and four young men, all in their late teens or early twenties, arrived at the door in anticipation of a good time.

Ned did all right with the introductions, brief and halting as they were, and seemed headed for some kind of acceptable performance when someone brought up the idea of a singing contest. The young ladies would accompany the young men at the piano, and the baritones and tenors would ply their talents for the entertainment of all. First up was Harry Phelps, an able young tenor whose repertoire included "Bicycle Built for Two" and "Sidewalks of New York." Then Walter Jenkins sang "Wait 'til the Sun Shines, Nellie" to loud applause. He was the clear favorite, even after Lloyd Marsh did a clownish rendition of "In My Merry Oldsmobile."

I watched Ned as the others took their turns, wondering how he'd handle this. It seemed too far fetched to think he'd sing at all, and I was right. When his turn came, he stood up, reddened, looked around like a trapped animal, and slid down to a sitting position against the wall. The group thought he was clowning and gathered round to laugh with him, but Ned wasn't laughing. He hugged his knees to his chest, swayed back and forth and crooned, "Soom, soom, soom, soom." The looks that passed around the room told the story. Ned MacPhail was done with this crowd. They thought he was strange, weird, queer, more than a little off.

Dampened by his obvious inability to run with the crowd, the party broke up soon after, leaving Ned to Beth and me. Only Catherine Townley, a bright young woman, though not overly attractive, stopped to whisper encouragement to Ned on her way out the door. The others couldn't be gone soon enough.

I stood by the door and waved them off with my best attempt at feigning polite apology. Beth took Ned by the arm and walked him back to the kitchen where plates full of party food lay untouched. Poor Ned. He stood looking down at the bounteous table, wiping the tears from his eyes. I'll tell you this about Ned MacPhail. He had courage. He'd tried manfully to fit in, to be one of the crowd, to be like everybody else, even though it terrified him.

"I'm sorry, Will. Sorry, Auntie Beth. I didn't mean to get so overwrought."

It was Sarah's word. She used it often in reference to Ned. Overwrought. "Don't do this, Ned. You'll get overwrought. Don't go there, Ned. You'll just get overwrought."

I took him by the shoulders and turned him to face me. "It's okay, Ned. You'll get it," I said softly. "We just pushed you too hard—too soon. You'll be fine one of these days. Just you wait and see."

I knew it sounded hollow, but it was all I could think of to say, and I really did hope it was true.

Ned turned away from my grasp. "No. I won't, Will. I'm different. I know that. Papa and Mama knew it, too. And Sarah. I get so scared when new people are around. Something happens to me. I shake inside. Maybe I better go back and stay in Mt. Etna. At least everybody knows me there. I guess they think I'm tetched, too, but at least they aren't afraid of me."

I leaned an elbow up against the wall and sighed. It hurt to see him hurt. I'd known him all his life. I knew how his family tried to protect him. I knew he wanted more from life, and I wished it for him, but I didn't know how to help him get it.

"Yeah. I guess so, Ned. If you feel more comfortable there, I'll take you home."

Chapter 10

Sarah, 1906

I didn't often venture far from home, but my curiosity about this new town, Blair Four, made me want to have a look-see, so on an August afternoon, after picking my pail full of blackberries, I veered off the railroad track onto the path to the village.

Wandering along at a leisurely pace, I heard talking and laughter off the path. It sounded like women or girls, so I moved toward them, curious. There, in a small opening in the woods, were gathered five women and about a half-dozen young children. Dressed in gaudy-looking bright colored clothes, the women sat on the grass, legs outstretched, skirts spread wide around them. The children ran about, pelting each other, wrestling, and playing some kind of tag game while their mothers talked and laughed among themselves. They seemed to be having fun, but I couldn't understand a word of their language. Some Slavic gibberish. They looked so happy, so content, even though their lot in life promised little. I knelt in the shelter of the trees and watched them for a few minutes before realizing that I was just like Ned, watching from afar.

Rising, I made my way back to the path and continued on to the village, coming out near the depot behind the store, the largest building, busy with people coming and going. To get a closer look, I mounted the concrete steps and entered a large, open room with a wooden counter stretched across one end. There, behind the counter, stood Phillip Chamberlain, in shirt sleeves with sleeve garters, wearing a green apron, waiting on a customer. I would have turned and run away, but he saw me and raised his hand in welcome. "Sarah! Hello! How nice to see you again!"

Astounded, I stopped, rooted to the spot, my heart pounding wild in my chest. What was this? Phillip Chamberlain, a store clerk? And talking to me as though nothing had ever happened between us?

"Phillip? What are you doing here?" My voice must have quavered. How could it not?

He stepped around the counter, smiling, to greet me as though I were an old and valued friend.

"I work here now. My uncle owns the store and he needed help, so I came on temporarily. Just until I hear from one of the colleges I applied to. Albright, Gettysburg, Lycoming. I should be hearing from one of them any day now. How've you been?" He smiled easily and touched my arm.

I reached behind me and grasped the rim of a barrel to steady myself. Phillip Chamberlain, working in a store at Blair Four? Really? And overjoyed to see me?

"Claire will be delighted."

"Claire? Here?"

"Yes, we're living in the quarters behind the store. Come, let me take you 'round."

He led the way out of the store, looked around to see that no customers were about to enter, and gestured for me to follow. I did so on shaky legs, still trying to gather all this in my mind. Phillip proceeded as though we'd only just been casual friends, glancing over his shoulder and smiling as we walked.

"Claire, Dear! Come see who's here!" His every move, every gesture evoked a sense of blamelessness, as though some invisible hand had wiped the slate clean.

Then Claire appeared in the doorway, a small girl clinging to her skirt. She smiled and extended a hand, though blushing at her reduced circumstances. The living quarters were modest and would have done nicely if cared for, but it appeared that Claire had no talent for housekeeping, as evidenced by the array of cluttered disorder that prevailed.

"Sarah. How nice to see you. I planned to come visit after we got settled, but the time just got away from me." She, too, acted as though our last encounter had never happened.

Jolted by the memory of that meeting, I must have frowned, for she brought her hands to her cheeks as though embarrassed.

I forced a smile and turned to Phillip. "You should get back before you miss a customer."

He nodded and hurried 'round to the front of the store, leaving Claire and me to make what we would of this happenstance. "So, what a surprise to find you two here at Blair Four."

She cleared a chair for me to sit. "Yes. It was a surprise to me, too. Phillip was let go at Juniata the year after our wedding. He said it was about the budget, but I always suspected there'd maybe been another—you know—liaison with a student. He's been trying to get hired at any number of colleges all over the state, but nothing yet. We were living with my parents in Lewistown until this came up. Not our idea of a permanent place, but we're sure something will materialize for the fall term."

I listened, trying to make sense of what she was saying. Another liaison with a student? Why was she telling me this? Hadn't I borne enough for my naïveté?

I turned to the little girl, anxious for a distraction. "And who is this young lady?" The child, about two, stood watching me warily from the safety of her mother's chair.

"This is Olivia, our second child. The first came along quite quickly after we were married, as children often do, but he only lived for three months."

"Oh, how sad for you."

Claire nodded, looking down at her dress front.

The child looked none too clean, her hair uncombed, her nose in need of wiping, her breakfast visible down her front. Claire looked tired and worn, and the house looked like a rag and bone shop. How the mighty . . .

"Sarah, I hope you don't still bear me any ill will. Marriage hasn't been all we'd hoped it would be, and, honestly, right now I need a friend."

"Oh, Claire, of course I don't. I could use a friend myself, so let's just let the past be the past and go on from here." It belied my true feelings, but somehow I felt sorry for this bundle of blighted hope.

She rose to fix us a cup of tea, all the while verbalizing her frustrations and disappointments as though meeting me had breached the dam and let the waters flow. "Don't regret not being married, Sarah. It's not as wonderful as we all dreamed. In fact, I hate it."

"Now Claire, surely you don't hate Phillip. It's just frustration with your situation. Once he's happily employed at a college, you'll be fine again."

"I wish I believed that. But, no. I'm pregnant again, and I'm afraid my life will be nothing but one baby after another and endless housekeeping. I know that's supposed to be our lot in life, but I can't help wanting more."

I stopped to consider this. Even though I might envy Claire's status as a wife and mother, I knew from the other women I'd seen growing up that a woman's lot was wholly dependent on who and how she married. My own mother was happy and content with father, but he was twice her age and had lost a whole other family before us, and I think that made him more appreciative of her and of us. Many women I knew endured abuse and overwork, bore children endlessly, and were expected to submit to whatever demands their husbands chose to exercise.

"But Phillip. Surely he's more, ah, . . . enlightened. Better educated. I mean . . ."

Claire shook her head. "Surely you remember how he used you. Well, we weren't married more than three months before his arrogance came to the fore. I was already pregnant—it was a difficult pregnancy and delivery—and Phillip showed no concern whatever for my well-being. He thought my mother should care for me and leave him free to pursue his own goals."

"Oh."

"Yes. Oh."

I felt some modicum of guilt, sitting there listening to her litany of complaints while still feeling resentment at the way I'd been treated, but it was clear she needed someone to listen—a sympathetic ear, if you will. We spent the better part of the afternoon with Claire sharing endless intimacies that I wished she'd kept to herself, before I finally rose to go.

"Oh, Sarah, please do come back soon. I'm ever so lonely here, with no one to talk to." She actually sounded almost desperate.

"Yes, of course, but you can come over to Mt. Etna, too. Bring Olivia along. We can have a nice afternoon. Mrs. Beck's granddaughter will be happy to watch her for you."

So I left her amid the Wreck of the Hesperus, her hair in disarray, her dress soiled and in need of a few stitches here and there, and the pot boiled over on the stove. Well, Sarah, I said to myself, be glad for wishes unfulfilled.

Back at the manor house, I sat down to write a few letters, wondering where Ned might be. The possibility of his wandering around Blair Four worried me, but I couldn't keep watch on him every minute. I cast about daily for something for him to do—a simple occupation that he could follow—one that might end in some sort of independence.

I talked to Richard Trethaway about Ned when we happened to meet, and, unfailingly sympathetic, he never wavered in his contention that Ned would be all right if left alone. I couldn't admit it to myself then, but Richard was my salvation in those years. Kind and always ready to listen, he took my problems as his own and studied them, looking for ways to help me manage the properties or handle Ned.

Ned still liked to go fishing, and, beyond his fascination with Blair Four, fishing was about the only thing that kept his interest. Seasonal though it was, I saw this hobby as something to occupy Ned's restless mind and, I hoped, distract him from associating with unworthy people. So I'd encouraged Ned to tie flies all winter, getting up a collection for the coming spring. He took to that, partially, I was sure, only because cold weather curtailed his ability to roam free in the direction of Blair Four.

His interest in fish never waning, Ned submitted to my encouragement in this other direction, and he began a collection of feathers, hooks and threads that he used to create imaginative insects to lure trout into getting caught. His first efforts were awkward and probably not very appetizing to the fish, but he kept at it through the winter months, and when spring arrived he set out to test his specimens.

His success was surprising, and whether it was the flies he'd tied or his native mastery of the local waters, it wasn't long before people were coming to the door asking whether they could buy some of Ned's flies. They were met, in typical Ned fashion, with a blank look, a silent shake of the head and a polite, if halting, refusal. Not to be put off, a few of the more zealous fishermen came asking me to spirit some of Ned's creations away for them and offering to pay well. That sparked an idea that I was anxious to put before Ned.

"There was a fisherman at the kitchen door this afternoon wanting to buy some of your flies," I told him at dinner.

"No. I don't want to sell them."

"Why not?"

"'Cause then people would come around all the time. You know I don't like strangers."

"Oh, yes, I know, but you could get around that by putting your flies out to sell at some stores—in Williamsburg or Alexandria perhaps."

Ned sat quiet for a while, chewing his hot roll and considering. "Would they give me money for them?"

"Yes, of course. You could make a nice tidy little income. Why don't you try it?"

"Could I keep all the money myself and spend it myself?"

"Yes, I think you should."

"Good. Then I could buy cigars and go have a beer at Water Street with my friends."

"Now, Ned, be reasonable. You know I don't approve of smoking and drinking."

He crossed his arms, leaning back in his chair. "Then I won't sell my flies. If I make money, I should be the one to say what I buy with it."

Stubborn determination lurked behind that open, innocent face. I sighed. "All right, then. You can be in charge of your own finances, but if I ever catch you smoking or drinking, I'll . . ."

A faint smile played at the corners of his mouth. His eyes twinkled just a little. "What will you do, Sarah? Paddle me?" He laughed out loud. "Whew, Sarie. Gotcha now!"

As it turned out, Ned gave me a felt of his flies the next day and I took them to Walker's General Store in Williamsburg, where they were displayed right next to the fishing rods, reels, nets and line. An instant hit, Ned became the recipient of a credit account at the store, where he could take his pay in goods. That lasted for a few months—until Ned got it in his head that he wanted real cash, so an arrangement was made to open an account for him at the bank and, in like fashion, Ned's independence was won.

Cousin Will found Ned's success heartening. Always an advocate for Ned, he chided me for being over-protective, even controlling. But I insisted, and still do, that Ned was an innocent in dire need of protection.

Chapter 11

Ned, 1906

I'm tired of people looking strange at me. I don't know why they think I'm odd or dumb or tetched in the head. I'm fine. I'm twenty-one years old and a man. I just wish I could convince Sarah. She thinks I'm a still baby that has to be watched all the time. It was better when Papa and Mama were still alive. They understood me and didn't try to make me do stuff I didn't want to do, like talk to strangers. I don't like to talk to strangers because I don't know what to say. I want them to like me and be my friends, but if you don't know them real well, you can't think of anything to say. So I just turn around and go the other way or cross the road so I don't have to talk to them.

And I don't like it when things get too loud or somebody tries to make me do something I don't want to do. It scares me, so I noddle. Noddle's what I do when I'm scared or lonely. I sit down on the floor, put my back against a wall, rock back and forth, and noddle. It makes me feel better, but people always try to make me stop it. I don't want to stop. It's the only thing that makes the scared go away.

Now Sarah won't even let me go fishing alone. Somebody always has to come with me, but a lot of the time there's nobody who isn't busy. Mama used to let me go fishing all by myself anytime I wanted. Now I have to wait until Richard Trethaway wants to go, and he only goes if he's done with his chores. He does chores all the time. My brother Andrew used to take me fishing, and he'd sit and watch the trains with me. He's a good brother. Better than Sarah. She's too bossy.

There's something else I like to do. I like to go over to Blair Four and watch them load the limestone on the trains, or watch the dinky cars bring the stone across the river from the quarry. And I like to watch Marta. Her pa works in the quarry, and so do her brothers, Andros and Josip. Her ma must be dead, 'cause the only girl I see over there is Marta. I think she's pretty. She does the house work and cooks and washes clothes.

I like to sit up in the tree beside her house and watch her. One time her brother Andros looked up and saw me. He yelled at me and made a fist. I don't understand their language, but I knew he didn't want me around there, so now I only go if her brothers are at work, and I go home before the workers get off their shift at the quarry.

Marta knows I'm there. She looked up and saw me in the tree one time and she just went on about her business, but she'd look up every now and again to see if I was still there. I like Marta. I'd like to talk to her, but I'm afraid, so I just sit up in the tree and watch. Her house is up on the higher street at the end, and my tree is on the side where nobody else can see me. I go over there about once a week, mostly on Wednesday, because that's not a busy day and there's usually no one around. Now Marta knows when I'll be there, and sometimes she looks up and smiles. One day she even waved to me. I waved back. She isn't afraid of me.

What bothers me is her father and brothers would probably beat me up if they knew I was still sitting up in that tree watching Marta. That one time I think they thought they'd scared me off.

They did, for a little while. But I watched to see when they were at work and when they were at home. I walk down the railroad track from Mt. Etna and cut through the woods to Marta's house, so nobody else knows about me and Marta.

Some day I'm going to talk to her—maybe show her my drawings of different kinds of trout. Brownies, Brookies or Rainbows. They're real pretty. That would be so much fun! But Sarah would be real mad if she found out.

I wish Will would come down for a visit. He hasn't been here in ever so long. Will's a doctor with Aunt Beth, and he's real busy, so he told me I couldn't stay with him anymore because he didn't have time to watch out for me. I was sad about that, mostly because it meant I'd have to go home and put up with bossy Sarah. I still like Will. He's always nice to me. He says I'm okay, just different.

I don't know how old Marta is. I'm twenty-one, and that's all the way grown—even if Sarah doesn't think so. I think Marta might be fifteen or sixteen. She's real pretty.

Yesterday I shook an apple down for her. Well, not really shook, see, it's an oak tree, not an apple tree. I brought the apple from home and dropped it down by her so she could get it. She did and looked up and smiled at me. Then she went in the house and didn't come out any more. It's getting cold now—October. I don't think I'll get to see her very much for a while. It'll be too cold to sit up in the tree all day, and once the leaves fall it won't be a hidey tree anymore.

Still, I think I might try to talk to her once. I whittled a fish out of pine, stained it with walnut hulls, painted it up like a Rainbow Trout and tied it on a strip of rawhide. I'm going to give it to Marta.

Sarah

I was just thinking I might be able to manage Ned, keep him under control, when one of the neighbor boys appeared at our back door one fall afternoon and told me Ned had been hanging around Blair Four again, sitting up in a tree watching some girl. I was in a dither over that, I can tell you. Sitting up in a tree? Watching what? Some dark-skinned, babushka-wearing little chippie with no upbringing and no English? Well, we would see about this. Right at that moment, Ned was sitting on the old canal bridge, dangling his feet over the edge, looking innocent.

"Ned MacPhail! Come here! Right here! This instant!"

He came over, slow and reluctant, head down as though I were going to beat him. Truth to tell, I might have if I'd had a good switch.

"You've been hanging around Blair Four again."

He frowned and looked askance at me. "Who told you?"

"I have my ways of knowing. Now, you listen to me. You stay away from there. Those Huns and Austrians aren't our kind of people, to say nothing of the Italians. They'll rob you and beat you up—maybe even kill you. Is that what you want? Why, they're not even civilized. All they know is drinking and fighting. I don't want you over there, do you hear?"

Ned nodded, head still down, eyes on his shoes. "But they're not so bad." He mumbled it under his breath as though he wanted me to hear it, but didn't want me to hear it.

"Not so bad? Ned, really. You don't know about people. You think everyone is nice and proper, like us. But those people are horrid. They couldn't buy good manners and breeding if they were a penny a bunch. All they know is working like dogs in the quarry. How do you think they got that kind of work? Because they were refined? Educated? Intelligent? Not on your life."

Ned turned away without asking again how I'd found out about his adventures. I was glad of that, for I'd asked Buddy Walsh, a neighbor boy, to keep an eye on him and let me know if he strayed. Buddy wasn't exactly an upstanding young man, but I figured him for a good watchdog.

Then, one afternoon in late October, Buddy came to my door again, urgency written all over his face.

"Miss Sarah, you'd better come quick. Ned's hurt." I dropped everything, hurried out the door and raced down the track toward Blair Four, afraid of what awaited me.

About a half mile from home I came upon my little brother, lying along the railroad tracks, looking like he'd been put through the sausage grinder. Said they beat him up for talking to their sister. Well, he'd gone and done it now. Got those Austrians turned against him.

"Talking? I'd wager it was more than talking." I inspected his face, arms, and as much of his back as I could with him lying in the cinders, unable to rise. "How bad is it?"

"I don't know. My chest hurts."

It was more than that. A black eye. Bruises all over. Cut on his shoulder—deep. like they'd stabbed him. What was I going to do? I turned to Buddy, who was standing aside and looking just a little bit scared. "Run and get Richard Trethaway to bring the wagon. He can't walk home." Buddy was off at a run, his too-large shoes clopping off his heels.

I stood twisting my handkerchief in my hands, concern furrowing my brow. "Hold steady now, Ned. We'll get the doctor."

"No. I'll be all right."

I let go an anguished sigh. What could he have done to deserve this? Why beat up an innocent boy for nothing? What kind of people were they, anyway?

Ned lay curled up on his side. It was getting late, so I could barely see the damage, but it was clear every effort to move brought pain. "Don't worry, Ned. Richard's coming to take you to the doctor."

"No. Just leave me alone."

"I can't leave you lying here to freeze overnight. You must tell me what happened."

I turned to see Richard striding along the path from the main road. I rushed to his side, babbling about Ned, almost incoherent. Richard listened for a few seconds, then knelt beside the helpless boy.

"What happened, Ned?"

"Nothing happened."

"Don't be silly. You were just out for a walk and a tree fell on you? Looks like you might have some broken ribs. Did they kick you?"

He nodded. "It was just them."

"Them? Who, them?"

"Marta's brothers."

"Who's Marta?"

"My girlfriend."

This revelation shed shook me to my roots. Marta was an Eastern European name—Serb, Croatian, something like that. Maybe Ned had fantasized himself a Slavic girlfriend and said or done the wrong thing. That was probably it. These foreign quarry workers were very protective of their women.

Richard bit his lip, shaking his head. "Your girlfriend? Come on, Ned. Where'd you get yourself a girlfriend?"

"Blair Four."

"I figured. So who beat you up?"

He winced in pain as he raised his hand to wipe his eyes. "Her brothers. Andros and Josip."

"Why?"

"They came home and caught us."

"Caught you? Doing what?" I drew in my breath. Oh, God, what now?

Now I really *was* worried. No telling what Ned took for courting. It was a sure thing these Slavic boys weren't going to allow it.

"Talking."

"Just talking?"

The story came out in halting chunks, separated by long silences and a few groans. He'd been watching this girl all summer, and she knew it. She didn't mind. She'd smiled at him and seemed to like him, so he climbed down from his tree and gave her a necklace he'd carved. A fish. It was the first time they'd tried to talk to each other, and since her English was so poor, they didn't get far. Far enough, though, that they were still standing in the yard looking at each other when her brothers came home from the quarry.

Without asking any questions, they proceeded to beat the tar out of Ned and knock him windless and dizzy. The message was quick and brutal. Stay away from our sister. Stay away from our town. They smashed the fish and threw it at him before leaving him sprawled across the railroad tracks with the warning: "No come back. No see Marta."

The picture slowly formed in my head. Ned, being Ned, climbing down shy and hesitant. The girl, also shy and aware of her family's rules, wanting to accept his gift but afraid. I could see them standing there, smiling into each other's eyes, their hearts pounding, shy, but drawn by a force beyond their ken. The brothers coming home to their little sister seemingly taken advantage of by some rich, privileged American kid. Recipe for disaster.

And a disaster it was. At my wits' end with trying to protect him, I wanted to send Ned away to some school or something. I fussed and fumed and wrote letters, but knew he was too old for boarding school, and college was out of the question. If it'd actually come to sending him away, I'd never have been able to do it.

I knew I couldn't, but I also knew we had to reach him somehow—get him to see the danger of what he was doing. God, Ned. What were you thinking?

But winter stole upon us, cold, dreary and confining, I dared to hope that Ned's beating had taught him a lesson no talking ever could. It took him the whole winter to mend, and when spring came, he turned his attention to fishing with no mention of his former troubles. He stayed around home, sought the company of Buddy, and seemed content with his limitations. Naïvely, I thought: lesson learned.

Chapter 12

Sarah, 1907

Now that I had a reason to go to Blair Four to visit Claire, I took advantage of the opportunity to look around the little town and judge for myself.

I must admit it was neat and tidy. The men all worked in the quarry, while the women took care of the children and the company house. It seemed orderly enough, but there was an undertone of uneasiness about the place. I attributed it to the difficulties of mixing peoples from different parts of the world without the benefit of a common language. But even though they didn't speak each other's languages, they managed to communicate well enough to work together, sing, dance, drink and fight. The fighting seemed continuous to one who wasn't used to violence, apparently the only means of settling disputes that talking might have served in a more civilized society. This uneasiness made me want Claire to visit Mt. Etna more often than I visited Blair Four.

Claire Chamberlain attached herself to me like a cocklebur. She visited as often as she could, walking down the railroad tracks with little Olivia in tow. We would sit in the parlor or on the front porch, drinking tea and talking, mostly about Claire's troubles. Her pregnancy would have made her seek refuge at home in more polite society, but living at Blair Four seemed to give her license to break the rules or neglect to follow them, which, to me, was the same thing. So she wandered about, blithely ignoring any constraints on the public appearance of pregnant women.

Her dissatisfaction with her life didn't diminish, and the longer she found herself confined to what she considered crude society, the more unhappy she became. She spoke little of Phillip, beyond the occasional report on his fruitless quest for a position worthy of his intellect and talents. I wondered at how one could turn from the wildest of infatuations to cold dislike in so short a time, but I couldn't disagree that Phillip was distant, callous.

Her time was coming in October, so she was forced to stay at home once the weather turned cold, and each time I went over there to visit she pleaded with me to come more often and stay longer. Then, one particularly chilly and blustery afternoon, Phillip Chamberlain appeared at our door with little Olivia at his side.

"Could you please look after Olivia for a while, Sarah? Claire's time has come. I've called into Williamsburg for the doctor and set some of the neighbor women to care for her until he comes."

"Certainly, Phillip. Is there anything else I can do? Come in, Olivia."

"No, thank you. I just hope this doesn't drag on like the first one did."

His demeanor seemed indifferent, as though the birth of his child was at best an inconvenience. He pushed Olivia in the door and turned to leave.

"I'll be back for her tomorrow."

I took the little girl to the kitchen, sat her up on the sink, and poured some warm water from the kettle. The child needed a good bath and clean clothes, but, of course, her father hadn't thought to bring anything. Mrs. Beck's daughter had little ones. Maybe we could find a change of clothes there.

Opting for a full bath, I pulled out the laundry tub and pumped more water into the kettle. While it heated I took off her dirty clothes—looked like they hadn't been changed in some time—and wrapped the child in a warm shawl Mrs. Beck kept in the kitchen. We played finger games and sang nursery rhymes until the bath was ready, and I found myself more than happy caring for the little waif.

Once bathed, her hair washed, dressed in borrowed, but clean clothes, Olivia looked like a different child. She climbed up in my lap and asked for a cookie, which Mrs. Beck provided, then curled up and went to sleep. Sitting in the kitchen rocker, holding her, I felt like a mother—a feeling I'd long since despaired of knowing.

Phillip didn't come for her the next day, or the next. After three days, I sent Buddy Walsh over to Blair Four to see what had happened. The boy returned with the news that Mrs. Chamberlain had been delivered of a baby boy after much laboring and difficulty. Mr. Chamberlain asked that I keep Olivia for a few more days until his wife regained her strength. I was sorry for Claire's difficulties but delighted to keep Olivia for as long as they needed me, and I sent word that Olivia needed some clothes if she was to stay longer. That evening a boy from Blair Four arrived with a bundle of clothes that turned out to be dirty, but at least the child would have something to change to.

Phillip Chamberlain's blasé attitude regarding his family amazed me. How could I have missed the flaws in this man's character? How could I ever have seen him as God-like, a perfect man to dedicate my life to? Now, far removed from those days, I smiled to think how lucky I'd been to have lost him.

I wondered at that. Surely, all men weren't so callous. I thought of Richard Trethaway, the only other man I knew very well, and decided, no. All men were not so callous.

***

The following June, after a very hard winter, I tried to visit Claire as often as I could, for her unhappy state worried me. I'd promised to go over to Blair Four to help her make strawberry preserves in June, so I tied on my bonnet, picked up a basket of jars and set out. My heart wasn't in it, but I forced myself to put aside the impulse to turn around and head for home, taking up one foot and putting down the other until I reached the village. I found Claire muddling around in her kitchen, the baby on her hip and little Olivia, with a dirty face and torn soiled dress, playing in the side yard. I didn't know what possessed Claire to have become so slovenly, but then, I'd never been to her mother's house in Lewistown, so maybe it was what she was used to.

"Here, Olivia, let me wipe your face." I took the child's hand and led her to the pump beside the house. "Would you like to pump the water for me?"

She stretched tall for the pump handle, just out of reach, so I lifted her up so she could apply every bit of little girl strength to raising it up and pushing it down. After three pushes, the water streamed out into the wooden trough. I reached for a cloth, wet it in the cold water, and wiped the child's face as she squirmed in protest.

It occurred to me that one had to rub hard to remove three days of dirt, but I set her back down on the ground without cleaning her ears, which sorely needed it. Claire watched, distracted, making no excuses for the sorry state of her house and children. She picked up a basket of strawberries harvested the day before and carried them and two pans to the little lean-to that served as a porch. We sat on two straight chairs capping strawberries, dropping the berries into one pan and the caps into the other, speaking but little.

Olivia played in the yard and the baby, wrapped up tight on this nice warm June day, fretted and fussed in a cradle pulled up beside his mother's chair. After watching him struggle and protest for some time, I told Claire, "I think he's too warm. Too confined. You should loosen his blankets so he can move—even take them off for a while."

Claire, oblivious to her children as usual, nodded absently. "I guess you can do that, if you wish. He's such a fussy baby, always crying about something. I haven't had a good night's sleep in the eight months since he was born."

I reached down, lifted the child into my lap and proceeded to unwrap the blanket. As I did, the baby quieted, and by the time he was free, he was smiling like the little angel he was. Again the feeling of envy flashed through my mind. Why should Claire, who clearly didn't want them, have two such healthy, rosy-cheeked children while I would remain childless? Why not I—who would care for them, keep them clean and safe? But hope diminished with the years. Where was I to find a husband in Mt. Etna?

I spread the blanket on the porch floor and laid the baby down. Now completely free of restraint, he extended his little arms and legs, as though freedom of movement were the greatest joy, turned over and got up on his knees, rocking back and forth in anticipation of getting around on his own.

Claire rose and entered the washing lean-to, put a kettle on the stove and deposited the berries in it, along with a full measure of sugar. Before long the scent of cooking strawberries wafted out to the porch.

Claire, standing before the hot stove stirring the berries as they thickened, seemed to want to talk. "Are you happy, Sarah?" she asked.

"Happy? I suppose so. I don't often think of happiness. There's so much to keep me busy, I guess I just get lost in the doing. You don't seem very happy now, but this has to be temporary. Surely Phillip will find a place soon and your fortunes will improve."

She stood watching the bubbling mixture, her face pensive. "No. I'm not happy—not at all. But I rather think this is the way life will be for me. Not what I expected and surely not what I dreamed of as a girl."

"What did you dream of? Perhaps if Phillip knew of your dreams, he'd do his best to make them come true. Think of it, Claire. You've everything a woman could want: a loving husband, two darling children, hope for the future."

She stood in the doorway looking out over the yard, her face blank. "Yes. Yes, I know I should be happy, but . . . The future? What of the future? More of this?"

She stood, head down, like a condemned woman sent to the gallows, her posture speaking depression. Why? I wondered. Why can't she find joy in her life? What would it take to raise her up out of this quagmire?

I rose and placed a hand on her shoulder, but instead of responding in kind, she shuddered and moved away. Just then Phillip appeared around the corner from the store, smiling as though everything in his world was fine.

"Sarah! How good to see you. You don't come by nearly as often as Claire would like. You two were such great chums at school."

"Yes, well, life keeps both of us busy, you know."

He stooped to tickle the baby under his chin while Olivia ran up to show him a buttercup she'd picked. Clearly, the contrast between Claire and Phillip went to the depths of them. The more Phillip's take on life was easy and light, careless, even oblivious, the more Claire's descended into darkness, threatening to drag even me down. That was the reason for the rarity of my visits. Too dark. Too deep.

Chapter 13

Ned, 1907

Marta's brothers kept a good eye on her after the beating, so once the weather warmed I still went to Blair Four, but not as often.

I still liked Marta. She was real pretty—and shy, like me. They built another house right beside hers, so my tree was between them and I couldn't watch from there anymore. Besides, her brothers might take to coming home at odd hours, so I just watched from farther away, hoping to catch a glimpse of her. She would look around for me when she came out of her house, and if she saw me, she'd smile and then turn away or go back inside. I knew she liked me, even though we'd barely spoken on that other day. It made my heart beat fast when I saw her, and I wanted to call her name, Marta—wanted to tell her my name was Ned. She was real pretty. For the first time in my life, I thought I could talk to a stranger.

One spring day I was walking in the woods on the other side of the river up Tussey Mountain, looking for mushrooms. I'd roamed the woods around Mt. Etna all my life, knew them like an Indian scout. There were a couple of fallen-down cabins over there, and I liked to look around the rotting logs for mushrooms. Sometimes I'd climb over them and try to remember the stories my father had told me about the people who'd lived there years ago.

The one farthest from the river was the best preserved, roof fallen in, logs sagging, but the fireplace and chimney, a corner wall, and part of the roof were still standing. That afternoon I was coming up from the lower ground, quiet in the wet leaves when out of the corner of my eye I saw a flash of red. It took me a moment to realize it was Marta, slumped on the ground in the corner of the cabin, her face buried in her arms. As I got close enough to look over the low wall, I spoke to her without thinking, just as though we'd always talked like old friends. "Marta, what's the matter? Are you hurt?"

She looked up at me, her eyes brimmed with tears, a mean-looking bruise across her cheek. She shook her head. "No. No talk." She waved a hand at me as though to brush me off.

I understood no, but I knew that wasn't what she wanted. I pointed to myself. "Ned. Ned help you."

"No." She shook her head again, looked around in fear and rose to her feet. "No. You go." Her voice quavered like she was scared.

I reached for her hand. She pulled away, but I spread my hands, palms up, to show her I meant no harm. As she wiped her tears a soft smile crossed her face. A wave of wonder swept over me. I could talk to her. I wasn't afraid. She needed my help and I could be her protector. A strange feeling settled on me. The nameless fears I'd struggled with all my life drifted away on her smile.

We sat down on a log, surrounded by the damp smell of the woods, and I reached out and touched the bruise on her face. "Who?" I asked.

"Papa."

"Papa? Why?"

Struggling with the language, she explained her father had beaten her because she liked to take long walks alone in the woods. He thought she was meeting someone—a boy—and he forbade her to leave the house. But Marta was stubborn to the point of defiance. She would walk alone in the woods if she pleased. She looked up at me, tear stained, her brown eyes playing soft against my face. I already knew I loved her.

That meeting in the cabin was the beginning of our real friendship. We sneaked away to meet there, talk and laugh together, share secrets and dreams. Marta was the first real friend I ever had. I couldn't wait to meet her at our hidey place and sit with her, talking back and forth as we pieced together a language of English, Slavic and hand signs. I told her about the latest fish I caught and showed her a felt with some of my flies pinned to it. She seemed to like me, and even though we both struggled to understand, she never seemed to find me strange. She smiled when we met, brought me cookies and listened as my newly loosened tongue poured forth all the thoughts and feelings I'd kept inside. As spring blossomed into summer, her English got better and my shyness faded even more, and we forged a bond that would bind us for life.

As her need for independence grew, Marta's father and brothers tried to tighten control over her. I knew all about that. I told her about Sarah and how I hated being bossed around all the time, watched and corrected. They saw Marta as Sarah saw me—slow, innocent, simple, childlike. I knew it wasn't true, but years of being seen that way were hard to overcome. Neither of us was slow or queer or tetched in the head. Marta was different, just like me. That was all.

We would meet at the ruined cabin a couple times a week, at different times, nothing regular, always careful. It was hard not to go there every day, for I longed to be with her all the time. She was so happy when we were together. I understood it was because of me and that made me feel special—real grown up. At home, Sarah still treated me like a baby, but she had other things on her mind, so as time went on and her attention was diverted elsewhere, she bothered less about me.

I helped Marta learn English, but she kept that from her father and brothers. They spoke their Slavic language at home, but lapsed into broken English when they didn't want her to know what they were talking about. She giggled when she told me they couldn't keep secrets anymore.

We went on meeting at our cabin for the whole summer and into the fall, moving ever closer, feeling ever more tightly bound. I wanted to marry her, and Marta said she wanted to marry me, but if she talked to her father about marrying anybody, he laughed and said she wasn't meant to be a wife. She was meant to stay at home and take care of her father and brothers. I knew what Sarah would say about us getting married, but I couldn't deny the need that rose in me every time we met, so I decided to go to Altoona to talk to Will.

I didn't tell Sarah I was going, I just took the train from Mt. Etna and got off at the train station in Altoona. I'd been there many times with my parents and with Sarah, so I knew the way to Will's house. I arrived, unannounced, at lunch time.

Lunch time in a busy doctor's office was a quick, pause between patients, and I found Will and Aunt Beth on stools pulled up to an examining table, eating soup and bread.

"Ned! Where'd you come from? Is Sarah with you?" Will stopped in mid-bite, his bread poised at his mouth.

"No. I came alone. I wanted to talk to you."

Will's eyebrows went up, but he pulled up a stool for me, and Aunt Beth cut off a slice of bread and buttered it.

"What is it, old man? Sarah gnawing at your guts again?"

"No. Not Sarah." I looked around at the company—Will, Aunt Beth and Mrs. Powell. "Can we talk later?"

"Sure, Ned. Just let me finish my lunch and we can take a stroll. I can spare some time this afternoon."

I munched on my bread, relieved.

Later, Will and I walked downtown toward the railroad station and the big Logan House hotel. "So what's on your mind?' he asked.

"I got a friend. A girl friend. I want to marry her, but I don't know how you marry somebody."

Will's eyebrows went up again. "A girl friend? Who?"

"Her name is Marta. She lives at Blair Four."

Will pursed his lips. "Marta, huh? From Blair Four? Does Sarah know about this?"

"No. She wouldn't like it."

"Hmm. I don't know how you could get married without Sarah knowing about it. Where would you live?"

"I could build us a house. Over on the mountain. We could live there."

Will rubbed his chin. That's what he did when he was thinking. "Tell me about this girl, Ned. Who is she? Does she like you, too?"

"Oh, yes. We like each other a lot. She's from far away—a place called Croatia. I don't know where that is—but they talk in a different language. I taught Marta to speak English. She's not too good yet, but we get along. She's real pretty." I told him all about our meetings at the ruined cabin. He knew about that. He said my Uncle John used to live there after the Civil War. I'd forgotten that.

It had started to rain, so we stepped inside the Logan House for a cup of tea to wait it out. We sat by a window and watched the rain drops pelt the cobblestones by the railroad track. A train chugged up and sat heaving on the track while passengers alighted under the protection of the depot roof. Will was full of questions about Marta and me, and I was happy to talk about us because I never could at home.

"You and Marta, you've never . . . ah, you've never kissed her, have you?"

"Oh, no. She's too shy. I wouldn't want to scare her. We just talk and sometimes we hold hands. I like having a girl friend."

"So, why don't you just keep on what you're doing? Why change things? It seems as though you're both happy as it is."

"Well, for one, if her pa and brothers knew about us, they'd beat me up again and keep her in the house all the time."

Will sat back in his chair, hands folded across his stomach. "How do you think they'll act if you get married?"

I bit my lower lip, looked out the window and sighed. "That's why I came to you. I don't know how to get married, and if we do, I don't know what they'll do."

Will tilted his head and looked long at me. "I guess, legally, you and Marta have a right to get married, but getting her family—and yours, for that matter—to accept it is going to be pretty nigh impossible."

"What can we do? Maybe we should run away. Maybe we should come to town and try to get jobs. I could work at the market and she could maybe get work at a boarding house or something."

Shaking his head, Will replied, "No. I think you should just keep on being friends. Maybe time will soften her brothers up. Even Sarah, maybe. But you'll run into a buzz saw if any of them find out now."

Disappointment flooded over me. I'd hoped Will would know what to do, but he just warned me about touching girls and what that could lead to. I already knew what it could lead to. Marta and I needed to be married.

The rain had stopped and we wandered outside. The big clock in the passenger shed struck three, and I went to the ticket window and paid my fare back to Mt. Etna. The train was already pulling into the station.

"I gotta go, Will. You'll keep this to yourself, huh?"

"Can't promise, Ned. I will, if it doesn't mean trouble for you, but if it does, ..."

I boarded the train, sadly aware that my trip to Altoona had come to naught. I was on my own, and I didn't know how to make my way. The train ride back to Mt. Etna was quick—even with stops along the way. I stepped off the train, crossed the tracks with my back to the manor house, and walked down to the river. We always kept a boat tied there, and I stepped into it and poled my way across, following the overgrown trail that led up to the cabin ruins. I stepped in, found some firewood scattered about, and built a fire. The crisp October days were already carrying us toward the dreariness of November. The corner logs formed a neat shelter against the wind, so I wasn't cold, but I was hungry.

Going home meant facing Sarah, who, I suspected, had already been alerted by Will of my dangerous activities. I felt so alone, felt the old fears sliding back, wondered why I'd thought I could be like everyone else. Then, out of the evening mist, Marta appeared, calling my name. I reached for her, pulled her down beside me, clung to her.

Her father had beaten her again, split her lip this time, all over her going off in the woods. I kissed the soft, bleeding lip, so sad for my precious Marta. I'd never even kissed her before, but now, overcome with desire, I kissed her again and again. Her lips felt warm and welcoming, and I needed her, wanted her more than I'd ever wanted anything.

I took off my coat and laid it on the ground near the fire, and Marta covered us up with her shawl. We lay in each others arms, trembling, but not from the cold. I rolled over beside her, kissed her again, unbuttoned her dress and touched her breast.

"It's all right, Marta. We'll be all right. We don't have anything to fear. I won't let them hurt you any more." I whispered. "I love you. I love you."

Chapter 14

Ned, 1908

Me and Marta got real close that fall. We'd meet every time we could at the cabin. I'd go and check every day to see if she was there, and she came if she could sneak away. I cleaned out the corner of the cabin, raked out the dead leaves and laid some stones so it would be clean and tidy. Then I swept out the chimney so it would draw and built up a fire. I even repaired the roof some so that when it rained we could sit nice and dry and watch it. It was a cozy place until winter set in. Then we went for weeks without seeing each other. Marta couldn't get out so much in the winter, but when she could it was like we were already married and this was our house.

I was so happy because with her I could just talk like anyone else. She was so nice and so pretty, it made my heart want to burst every time I saw her coming through the woods to meet me. I wanted it to last forever, but I guess nothing lasts forever. That's what Sarah says, anyway. And Will. I guess they know more about things than I do.

All I know is that one day the following spring, Marta didn't come. I wasn't sad that day because I thought she'd come the next. But she didn't come the next day or the day after that. I started to feel real scared and sick in my stomach. I was afraid her pa and brothers had found out about us and had locked her up so she couldn't get out and come see me. I worried every day for five days, and then I had to go to Blair Four and see what was wrong.

I came into the village from across the river on the foot bridge that ran along by the bridge they brought the rock out on. It was a railroad bridge, up high on big stone supports in the middle of the river, with steel rails going across. The Dinky cars were loaded up with rock and brought over to the crusher and the kiln on our side. But the workers crossed on the wood foot bridge, so that's the way I got back to Blair Four from the mountain. Marta never used the foot bridge to come to me. Everyone in Blair Four would have seen her, so she took a path upstream and waded across a shallow part, holding her shoes in one hand and gathering up her skirt with the other. I'd watched her cross back from our cabin lots of times—watched so she'd get back all right.

When I got to the other side, I had to pass the rock crusher, a great big, loud machine that took the big rocks and smashed them down into pieces. I didn't like having to pass through there because the noise upset me. I don't like loud noise, and the workers around the crusher yelled at me and made mean hand signals. I walked past there as fast as I could and down the track toward the village. All the trees around there were covered with dust and when it rained they got all chalky and white water dripped off the leaves.

The village seemed normal—a little quieter than usual, but it was a warm, spring day and everyone went to the river when it was warm. The women would wash their clothes and the children would play in the shallow water. I could hear them as I curved up around the end of the upper street to look down on Marta's house. I sat down and watched for about an hour, I guess, and nobody came out or went in. The house just sat there, quiet. I was already upset because Marta didn't come, so I could hardly stand to just sit and watch. I started to noddle some—real quiet, sitting there on the hillside. I hadn't done that in a long time, but I was real scared and I needed comfort.

After all that time, the sun went down behind the trees and the men were coming home from work. The village came alive with sounds and smells. Mothers cooking supper, kids playing in the dooryards, fathers coming home covered with dust, washing, shirtless, at a basin on the porch. I climbed the big oak tree behind Marta's house and watched her brothers file in from work. The trees hadn't leafed out much yet, so I climbed up real high, where I could just barely see the dooryard. There wasn't any noise, no cooking smell, no papa coming home. I stayed up in the tree until after dark, sure there was something wrong in Marta's house. Then I saw the door open and Andros and Josip walked out, toward the railroad. I climbed down and went up to the door and knocked, a cold chill running down my back. I waited a long time, but no one opened the door.

So I made my way down to the lower street, looking for anyone I might know. People were sitting outside their houses. I could see the glow from cigarettes and hear them talking in low murmurs. I'd never walked up and talked to a stranger in my life, but I did that night. Shaking and stammering I stopped a man walking down the street, smelling of liquor.

"Excuse me, sir. Do you know what happened to Marta, the girl who lives up there?" I gestured toward Marta's house.

"Old man died," the man growled. "Three day ago." He stood unsteady on his feet, pulled his head back and looked at me closer.

"You the one done it?" he asked.

"Done? Done what?"

"Give her the round tummy. You know. Put a baby in her."

Astounded, I looked at him as though he'd accused me of murder.

"No. No. I never did that. I like Marta. I wouldn't . . ."

"Well, somebody did, and her pa and brothers figured to get him, whoever he was, but the old man got hisself scalped by a flying rock in the quarry. Lasted a few days, but that was it. Don't know what the brothers'll do now."

Taken with a sudden urge to run, I pushed past him, down the path toward the depot, past the store and out onto the railroad track. I turned toward Mt. Etna and kept running until I got home. I went in the kitchen and crept up the back stairs, but Sarah had ears like a bat and was waiting for me by my bedroom door.

"And where have you been all this time?" She asked it like she already knew where I'd been and with who.

"No place," I stammered. "I was just down at the river. Fishing."

"Fishing? Until ten o'clock at night? I don't think so. Don't you want any supper?"

I should have been starving, but the thought of food made my stomach churn. "No. I'm not hungry. I want to go to bed."

She blocked my way, but I moved her aside and entered my room. She stood outside my open door, hands on hips, head jutted forward.

"You can lie all you want, Ned MacPhail, but I know what you've been up to. Well, we've seen the last of that band of thugs. Come around here and demand money from me to keep them from killing you. I paid them off royally, so we won't be hearing from them again. I hope you realize the trouble you've caused trying to prove you're a man. Well, I guess you are, but you'd better forget you ever met that little chippie."

I stood in my room back against the door and slid down to the floor. I held my head in my hands, knees to my chest and rocked back and forth. Soom, soom, soom, soom, the sound coming out more like a moan.

Richard

First thing this morning, while I was still sitting at the breakfast table, Sarah MacPhail came rushing in, her face red from running, her skirts in either hand.

"Sarah, what is it? Did something happen?"

"Something certainly did. Do you remember those Austrian boys who beat Ned up for looking at their sister?'

"The Rodich boys? Sure I remember them. Why?"

"They came to my door yesterday and demanded to talk to me. Told me, in their broken English, that Ned had been seeing their little sister—*little sister,* they called her—and that she was with child! I couldn't believe my ears, Richard. Why, Ned! How would Ned ever get to know anyone—let alone a girl—well enough to . . ."

"Whoa. Back up. Ned? With a girl? I mean, I knew he liked that girl—liked to watch her from a tree, but when did he come down from the tree and start courting?"

"I don't know, for the life of me. But these young men, these Rodich boys, were adamant. They said if I didn't pay them off and pay well, they'd beat it out of Ned. Can you imagine?"

I must admit, I was dumbfounded. I hadn't seen much of Ned lately, and when I did, he seemed like the same old Ned, talking fishing endlessly. I'd never have credited him with the courage or the inclination to pair off with a girl. Shows you what *I* know.

"Are they sure it was Ned? How do they know it wasn't somebody else and they're just blaming it on Ned so they can get money?"

"They said the girl told them it was Ned. They'd been watching her—they say she's slow, too, like Ned—and they started to wonder that she was gaining weight. It took them some time to find out what was going on. Had to get a neighbor woman to talk to her, but talk she did. Said they had a place where they met and did things. I paid them off to get rid of them, but I just hope that's the end of it. Honestly, Richard, I don't know what I'm going to do with him. What if he does this again? I can't go paying people off forever."

"Slow down there, Sarah. Have you talked to Ned? What's he got to say?"

"He won't talk to me. He's in his room, rocking and keening like some Tibetan monk. Came home late last night after he'd been to Blair Four and found out everything, defiant as ever."

Sarah's chin quivered as she dabbed at her eyes with a handkerchief. I really did feel sorry for her, but I didn't know how to help her. I reached out a tentative hand and patted her on the shoulder.

"I'm sorry, Sarah. This is more than you should have to bear, but I hope now you realize Ned isn't as slow and childlike as you see him. He wants so much to be free and independent. I still think he'd get along on his own if you could let him."

She reached up and covered my hand with hers. "Ned's a good boy. He just doesn't know how to get about in this world."

"Have you talked to your cousin Will?"

"Oh, yes, many times. Not about this yet, but he knows how I struggle with Ned. I really think I might have to put Ned in some kind of home. I can't handle him anymore."

"Oh, no, Sarah. No. Don't do that. It'd be the end of him. Maybe this'll bring back his old fear of strangers. It certainly has to have scared him."

We walked out of the cottage into the morning sunlight, Sarah still wiping tears. We'd always been friends, Sarah and me, and I'd always wished it were more. I didn't make any assumptions, but I did nurture the hope that someday, maybe. But some folks would have thought I was trying to get the MacPhail money, so I kept to myself. The MacPhail money was long gone, if I was any judge. Sarah kept it together from rents and selling off parcels when she had to, but I knew it hurt her to do that. She had a lot of pride, Sarah did.

"You want me to talk to him? Maybe he'd listen to me."

"Please do, Richard. I've run out of patience and don't know what else to do. He can be so obstinate."

"All right. I'll stop over after breakfast."

"Oh, do come to the manor house for breakfast. I doubt Ned will come down today."

At the manor house, Sarah invited me to sit at the dining room table. That was a change. I'd always entered by the kitchen door, and if Mrs. Beck offered me a piece of pie, it was at her work table in the kitchen. I sat down and waited for Sarah to give her instructions to Mrs. Beck. It felt so strange to be sitting at that long, walnut table usually reserved for family or special guests, that I had to get up and look out the window. When Sarah returned, I asked if it was all right to go up and talk to Ned. She nodded, her eyes tearing up again.

I went out of the dining room into the center hall and up the wide stairway. I didn't know which door was Ned's and he didn't answer my call, so I opened the doors one at a time. A fool could tell which room was Ned's—clothes on the floor, the candle still burning down to a nub, the window open with the curtains blowing. I looked around the room. Empty. Ned was gone.

Chapter 15

Ned, 1908

I got up real early and left the house before Sarah was up. I didn't even know where I was going. I just wanted to be away by myself. I walked all the way to Williamsburg along the railroad track, but when I got to the square, I didn't know why I'd come. I wanted to get a job and live on my own and somehow get Marta to come and be my wife. The only place I knew there were jobs was in the quarries, and Sarah always said to stay away from the quarries. They were bad places full of bad people and bad things happened there. But I really needed a job, so I forgot about Sarah.

There was a man standing in front of the steps outside the general store, so I took a deep breath and went up, eyes downcast, and asked him if he knew of any jobs in the quarries. He grunted and pointed me back to the railroad. "Ganister. Keep on goin' the way you was. Down the track. Ye'll git there."

Ganister wasn't far out of town, down a little piece and across the river. There was a store and a lot of houses and a church with a funny looking thing that looked like a big, gold onion on the tower. I wondered why anyone would want to put an onion on their church. The rest of the town was a lot like Blair Four or Carlim—just houses, a store, people coming and going, dust everywhere, but strangely quiet that day.

I stood looking around with no idea of where to go and who to ask. A group of men loitered outside the store, looking sullen, but nobody paid me much mind. One man threw a questioning glance my way, but didn't care to ask who I was or what my business was. I went into the store, 'cause that's where I thought I could find out where to go to get a job, but once inside, I lost my nerve to talk. It was always like that. I got a crawly feeling in my stomach and my butt was full of pins and needles. Here it came—the urge to run. I bolted out of the store, back across the bridge and down the dusty track past a couple rows of houses, with no idea where I was going. It'd taken all the nerve I had to get to Ganister, and now I couldn't even ask anybody where I could find a job.

I wandered down the track that I thought led to the quarry, stumbling along, head down, eyes on the ground. Suddenly a rough hand grabbed my shoulder and swung me around. A fist smashed into my face, so hard my head snapped clear back on my shoulders. I saw a blot of red, a flash, and then nothing. The next thing I knew, I was lying on my stomach in the dust along the track, my face aching and my head about to burst. There was nobody around. I lay there for about five minutes before some other man came along and kicked the sole of my boot.

"On yer feet! Git up now. This ain't no place for sleeping off a drunk. Git on with you."

"I wasn't drunk. I . . ."

"Look, kid, I don't give a rip what your story is. This is a working quarry and we're on strike. Git up and git outta here before somebody takes you for a scab. Looks like somebody already has. Now git!"

I got up on my knees, swaying dizzy, but the man didn't wait for me to recover my balance. He gave me a swift kick in the butt that sent me sprawling again. This time I skinned up my hands pretty bad on the gravel. I rolled over on my back, as he lunged at me once more.

"I told you to git gone. You look like a nice enough kid. Don't belong around here. Now git gone before somebody breaks your stupid skull."

I raised a hand to parry another blow, fully expecting one, but the man just stood over me, fists clenched, glaring.

"Work. I wanted work."

"Oh, yeah you wanted to work all right. Work for nothing so a man who's got a wife and kids can't make enough to keep 'em. Goddamn scab."

"Scab? What's a scab? I just want a job."

"Take yer sorry ass some place else before you get it broken around here. We got no time for no scabs."

"Okay. I'm going. Don't hit me again."

I got up, the world still whirling, picked up my cap, slapped the dust off it and started down the road the way I'd come. As I crossed back to the railroad tracks, I saw a bunch of quarrymen standing down by the river, holding up a crude sign that said STRIKE! in big bold letters.

One of them shook a raised fist, but I'd had enough. I kept going, stumbling along as fast as I could, looking neither to the right or the left. Ganister was no place I wanted to be. I reached up and touched my jaw, moved it from side to side, felt it snap back into place. It hurt to open my mouth and I couldn't even stop to pick the gravel out of my hands as I lurched back toward Williamsburg.

Walking along the railroad track back through town I thought about what had happened. Maybe Sarah was right. Maybe I wasn't right in the head. I always thought I was, and Mama and Papa said I was but now I thought they were just trying to protect me. Sarah, too, only I didn't want to be protected. I wanted to be like everybody else, only I wasn't. I had to face that. I really was different.

Not stupid, not tetched in the head, just different, but that was enough to make my way in the world a hard one. It always had been, but living at Mt. Etna I could avoid other people and tell myself I was okay. If I wanted a real life, I had to get away, get a job, prove myself. The thought of it gave me a chill—two chills, really. One for how great it would be to be out on my own, working and married to Marta, and one for the cold, empty, leaden fear all that brought to the fore.

I trudged along the track back toward Mt. Etna, hands in my pockets, head down, my jaw aching. When I looked up and saw someone coming the other way—far down the track, my first impulse was to step off and head for the woods to avoid an encounter. I gave in to the urge, telling myself I must look a fright, embarrassed to be seen so beaten up. I stepped off the railroad and sneaked away about a hundred feet into the woods, squatting behind a bush. A honey bee buzzed around my head, then moved on to a clump of Black-Eyed Susans. Whoever was coming took their time, but I crouched and listened to the steady tramp of their feet on the cinder track. I breathed quiet and waited, and just as the man was abreast of me, he stopped.

"That you in there, Ned?"

"Richard. Yeah, it's me."

"Thought so. Come on out. Your sister's worried sick about you."

I rose from my crouch and stepped back onto the track. "Hello, Richard."

He nodded, took a look at my battered up face and whistled low.

"Looks like you've been mixing it up with those Austrians again. Looks like they won."

I nodded in shame. "They always win. I don't know how to fight."

"Guess not, but then you haven't had occasion to practice much."

He touched my jaw, turned my head from side to side, frowning. "So, you and Marta had a tryst, did you?"

"What's a tryst?"

"A tryst is what you and Marta were doing out in the woods, and what comes of that is a baby."

"Yeah, I guess I know that. I knew it from being around the farm, but I didn't think Marta would . . ."

"So you can't blame her brothers for being mad, now, can you? They think you took advantage of their little sister."

"But I love Marta, and she loves me. Why can't people just leave us alone?"

"Because you and Marta don't have an ounce of good sense between you. Sorry, Ned, but that's the truth. When they made you and when they made her, they left something out. Not everything, but something. And what they left out was what it takes to live with other people and get along."

I sat down on a cold steel rail, head in my hands. "I know I'm different, but I'm good and I'm smart. Why isn't that enough?"

"It should be, but if you're going to step off into the woods every time a stranger happens by, you might as well stay in Mt. Etna and live the life you were born to."

His words hurt. I knew he didn't mean them to hurt, but I also knew they were true. There was a lot I didn't get in life—mostly about other people—and I was pretty sure that wasn't going to change, even if I wanted it to.

Richard sat down on the rail beside me and draped a heavy arm over my shoulders. "You got any idea how hard it is to make a living and raise a family? This first little bundle you got going would soon be two, then five or eight. Takes a lot of hard work to raise a kid. Maybe you'd best let that to other people and just be who you are, like God made you."

"I think God made a mistake."

"He does, sometimes, but there's no explaining it or changing it. We all gotta be who we are, Ned. There's just no other way."

I got up off the rail and looked out at the river, the Blue Juniata, flowing along in the late afternoon sun, light glinting off the riffles and the water gurgling softly as it lapped the bank. The river always soothed me. I turned to Richard.

"I guess I better get on home. Sarah will be worried."

Sarah

Richard urged me not to worry where Ned had gone. He said he'd find him and bring him home, and for me to just go about my business and not let on to the villagers. He said they'd probably know all about it soon enough, but for now he didn't want any help in tracking Ned down. I agreed. It'd always been family practice not to share our private business with the world, so I tried to go on that day as though it were just like any other.

Somehow I knew in a distracted way that Ned would be all right, and that it wasn't incumbent on me to direct his every move. That was a bitter pill, for I took protecting Ned as a duty and an identity, but he'd certainly demonstrated his ability to work around me, so maybe I *should* step aside and let him become what he would. Right then it seemed clear he was old enough and bright enough to figure things out on his own, present circumstances notwithstanding.

When he came home that night looking much the worse for wear, I wanted to fuss over him, tend to his wounds, but he waved me off. "I'm okay, Sarah. Really. I don't need you to worry over me."

Just right, little brother. Just right. It was beginning to dawn on me that I couldn't live his life for him, couldn't protect him, couldn't be his guardian angel forever. I can't say I embraced the thought right away, but it'd been planted, for sure. I could never abandon him entirely, but I was beginning to think I should loosen my grip, just a bit.

I listened to his tale of woe, inspected his jaw, determined it wasn't broken, gave him a pat on the butt and sent him to the kitchen for some supper

Chapter 16

Richard, 1910

It was a bright sunny Sunday in August, welcome after a week of heavy rain. The river was swollen to the point that crossing by boat was too risky, especially with the number of children to be transported, but the bridges still held, so the Sunday School picnic for Blair Four Church was held on the Tussey side of the river, folk carrying their picnic hampers across on the foot bridge. Everyone in town was there, including me and a few other Mt. Etna folk who'd managed to form friendships with the quarry workers. There were sack races and archery contests and even a few wrestling matches which resulted in cheers for either participant and for once, no hard feelings about the result. Food was abundant—not the kind of repast I was used to, but very pungent and tasty nevertheless.

An itinerant minister who served Mt. Etna and Blair Four presided over the festivities with good will. Standing away from the rowdy party-goers, I noticed a small, dark haired, dark eyed girl—Marta Rodich—obviously with child. She looked sad. Personally I thought the Rodich boys and Sarah should just butt out and let Ned and Marta do for themselves, but that wasn't likely.

As the afternoon waned, people started to pack up and file back over, in twos or threes, spacing themselves to balance the weight on the rope suspension bridge, only a few feet above the roiling water. I was standing at the river bank chatting with a friend when Phillip Chamberlain's wife stepped out onto the bridge, carrying their baby boy. Phillip came along behind, holding the little girl's hand, and stopped to talk to me. I sold flour to the Blair Four store and he wanted to place an order for the next week.

Suddenly a tearing sound and a scream ripped the air as the bridge failed, dropping Mrs. Chamberlain and the baby into the rushing waters. I gasped and reached for the shredded rope, but the swift current had already carried them out of reach. We stood helpless on the river bank as the woman and child bobbed and sank, then bobbed up again, frantically flailing for help. The baby disappeared, while the mother was carried downstream, helpless against the driving current.

Phillip let go of the little girl's hand and ran toward the bank as though to jump in, but bystanders grabbed and held him fast. He struggled but couldn't break away, watching his wife and child disappear in the muddy, raging water. It was over in less than a minute—Claire carried far downstream, out of reach, the baby nowhere to be seen. The crowd stood in silent disbelief while some of the men rushed along on foot, hoping the woman would somehow manage to grab a snag and save herself. We stood watching the creamy brown turmoil swirling and racing away from us, with no sign of the lives it had stolen.

With the footbridge out, people had to climb up to the rail bridge and make their way carefully back across to the town, balancing on the rails or clinging to the ties until boards were brought and laid between them. The operation took the rest of the afternoon, while a rescue party ventured out on the raging water in a vain attempt to find the woman or the child. They gave up the search when they couldn't even touch bottom with their poles, oars were useless, and the would-be rescuers were carried far downstream before they could navigate to calmer waters.

After I'd helped get the last of the people across I walked down the track to the Blair Four store, where a crowd had gathered in front of the residence. Phillip sat on the porch in a wooden rocker, the little girl in his lap, a vacant look in his eyes.

"I told her to wait. Told her I'd be with her in a minute, but she would go on ahead."

"But then, you'd *all* have died." A man in the crowd tried to offer comfort.

"No. I'd have seen the ropes were frayed. I'd have noticed. Claire was in a huff."

I stood back listening, not wanting to offer advice or conjecture. It was a tragedy, not to be blamed, rationalized or justified. But people *would* talk. I looked at the child, huddled, afraid, in her father's lap. After a few minutes I stepped forward.

"Would you like me to take Olivia over to Sarah MacPhail? I'm sure she would take care of her until . . ."

"Yes," Phillip said absently, moving her to the ground. "Yes. Ask Sarah to care for her."

I took the little girl by the hand and started to walk toward the railroad track that led to Mt. Etna.

"I want my mommy," she sniffled, tears streaking her little face as she ran to keep up with my stride.

I stopped, picked her up and held her close. "It's all right, Olivia. Sarah will take care of you."

As I walked along carrying her, she snuggled up to my neck, an occasional sob shaking her little body. She caught the edge of my collar and held fast, her thumb solidly in her mouth. I wiped away a tear and held her closer to ease her three-year-old fears.

Sarah had heard of the tragedy by the time we arrived at the manor house after dark, and she rushed out to meet us by the canal, carrying a blanket to wrap about the little girl.

"Olivia. Come, dear child, I'll take care of you. Are you hungry? Would you like something to eat?"

I handed her off to Sarah, and she carried the child inside where she dished out a bowl of porridge covered with warm milk. She sat beside the child while Olivia ate, stroking her hair and whispering how happy she was that she'd come to visit. Then she carried her upstairs and tucked her into a trundle bed in the old nursery, knelt beside her, and sang a lullaby until she fell asleep.

Ned and I stood watching her nurture the poor waif, impressed with her motherly instincts, before we went down to the parlor to talk over the day's events.

"Why did she go out on the bridge without Phillip?" Sarah wanted to know. "Surely, she must have seen the ropes were frayed."

"Guess we'll never know the answer to that. Anyway, people were crossing back and forth all day. Could have been anybody."

Sarah turned away, wiping her eyes. "Claire was so sad. I wonder if she saw the frayed ropes and went out anyway."

I rose and went to her, took her hand, and sat down beside her on the velvet settee. "No, Sarah. No. Don't think that. It just happened. No one's fault. Could have been anybody." But I knew she had her own take on the tragedy, and who was I to dispute her?

The body of the baby was found the next day on the town side of the river, not far from the fallen bridge, but Claire's body lay a mile downstream, undiscovered for three more days. By that time it was necessary to bury her quickly, so a makeshift funeral was gotten up, attended by most of the Blair Four folk, and the body was transported to Lewistown for burial. Through it all, Phillip Chamberlain wandered, vague and displaced, unable to express any but the basest emotion. He moaned, groaned, and cried out in anguish—but never once asked about or showed any concern for his daughter.

When he returned from Lewistown a week later to gather his possessions and leave Blair Four, I went to the store to speak to him.

"What about Olivia, Phillip? Sarah MacPhail can care for her as long as you want her to, but your child needs you." I stood outside the residence, watching two local men load the wagon for him. He looked at me vaguely, as though the shock had rendered him senseless.

"Olivia. Yes. I've nowhere else to send her. Ask Sarah to keep her until I get settled somewhere."

I stopped by Mt. Etna with that message and no other word— no promises, no instructions, no regrets. Sarah took it in stride, maybe tinged with a little joy, for I already knew she loved the child.

Chapter 17

Richard, 1909-11

Funny how one event can change the whole direction of your life. Sarah with little Olivia, Ned with his new understanding of himself and his place in the world. Things leveled out for both of them in different ways. Taking in Olivia turned Sarah's life around—for the good. Motherhood was as natural to her as swimming to a duck. She opened her home and her heart and never gave it a second thought. It was good all around, too. The little girl thrived in Sarah's care, Ned got out from under her domination and Sarah got a purpose for her life.

Little Olivia became the center of manor house life, sweet child that she was. Sarah delighted in sewing dresses for her and doing her hair up in fancy curls. She taught the child impeccable manners and beamed with satisfaction when Olivia remembered to say please and thank you and excuse me. It was as though Sarah had always been destined to be a mother, and Olivia fulfilled the dream to perfection.

Now that Sarah was too busy to bother with him, Ned went his own way, fishing, roaming the woods, staying out of the way of strangers, not so shy any more, just preferring his own company. I heard from Blair Four that Marta Rodich gave birth to a boy child in October of '07. Named him Jacob. Jacob Rodich. I told Ned about him. Figured he had a right to know, but he didn't seem to want to go back there, seemed at peace with the facts. Jacob would grow up over there in Blair Four among the Austrians, unaware of the other half of his heritage.

Little Olivia turned six about a month ago and will be enrolled at Mt. Etna school for the fall term. Her father never even came back here for a visit. I guess that would have scared the daylights out of Sarah, though—the fear that he'd want the child back. Phillip Chamberlain got the job he longed for—teaching at some college down east, but he forgot all about his daughter. Just like that. A family splinters into kindling at the swing of an ax or the fall of a bridge.

So there was change in Mt. Etna—both good and not so good—for Sarah watched her fortunes decline as money was paid out to keep the place up and little came in to refill the coffers. The plantation had once held thousands of acres, but ever since the passing of small family-owned iron furnaces, the MacPhails had been forced to sell off parcels of land just to keep their taxes paid. Sarah talked about it to me, but there didn't seem to be any easy solution.

"I'm worried, Richard. I can't seem to find a way to keep it together."

"Well, I guess you could sell some—just a few acres here and there. I wouldn't let any large tracts go." I was uncomfortable with the whole prospect—the kind of change I didn't like to think about.

"Well, there's still a lot of land over on Canoe Mountain. I guess I could sell that. Taxes are high and getting higher, and I get so little income from these properties. It costs more to keep them up than they bring in."

"You could rent some land to farmers. Sell an acre or two for building lots."

"What bothers me most is the deterioration. It's great to own something until it comes to keeping it up. These buildings sitting around unused are simply going to rot."

I wished I could come up with an idea—some plan that would take care of everything for her. Truth was, the old place was a liability. That was hard for Sarah to accept, but it was true.

"I'm so afraid that I'll be the one to let it all go—that it will come down to me—everything the generations before worked so hard to build, and I won't be able to hold on."

I watched over the years as her holdings diminished, pained at the prospect that she might be right. Like Sarah, I loved the place and couldn't just stand by and let it all go.

Right around the early part of the new century, a group of town folks bought up riverfront lots for a little summer camp called the Sycamore Cottages. Sarah liked the kind of folk that brought in—town people with a little money and a taste for the finer things. She'd entertain the cottage people of a summer evening, delighted to share her love of reading and poetry.

The whole village blended into one America on the Fourth of July when Olivia and the other youngsters from both communities would make up a little parade with bunting-draped goat carts and march through the village singing Yankee Doodle to the accompaniment of an ancient fife and drum. The cottage folk brought a welcome air of gentility that had been lacking for Sarah ever since her parents died.

I knew the finances were strained, but Sarah still cared a lot about keeping up appearances, so she continued what she called her genteel ways—store bought hats and coats for Olivia, a pony and cart, shopping trips to Altoona. In spite of her efforts to keep things up, the old plantation took on a seedy look. Weeds where there'd once been pasture, rocks falling away from the old structures, roofs in need of repair. Keeping up a place like that took a lot of hands, and Sarah's and mine and even Ned's were never enough.

Sarah

As time went on, I came to the reluctant realization that my money was simply running out. I resisted the idea of selling anything, but when the taxes for one year weren't paid and the tax bill for the next year arrived, I knew I had to do something, so I contacted Gilbert Dean, a realtor from Hollidaysburg, and invited him to Mt. Etna just to talk. We went over the whole estate, listing the properties, boundaries and condition. It was hard for me. I loved every inch, every blade of grass, every worn out, falling down structure. But there it was. I had to do something, so I listened to Mr. Dean's proposal.

"I think you'd do best to sell that whole section up Roaring Run. The barn, the old store and office building, the tenant house, the blacksmith shop, the little house, the furnace—all of it, with about twenty or thirty acres of ground."

"Oh, no. That's too much. I can't part with all of that. Not the little house. That's where my Grandma Ellie lived. And the furnace? It's an historic landmark. I can't let that go."

Mr. Dean sat back, steepling his fingers, and waited as I recited my lamentations. He let me say all I had to say, then leaned forward in his chair. "Miss MacPhail, you have staggering liabilities here. The roof of the barn is ready to fall in, the blacksmith shop is a ruin. Even if you wanted to rent out the tenant house, you'd have to do extensive repairs. If I were you, I'd get rid of every thing, sell the manor house, and get out. Go to town. Buy a nice house. Raise your little girl there. This place is going to get worse every year."

"No. I was born and raised in Mt. Etna. I'll never leave it, and I won't sell the furnace or the little house—or the tenant house. And that barn. It used to house a hundred mules in the iron making days. It's a stone bank barn. There are only a few of them left. I can't sell it."

He sighed and pulled out a form. "All right. Exactly what *do* you want to sell?"

I thought about it for a while, trying to maintain my composure. "The barn and the store, but that's all."

He listed the properties and did some calculations, filled out the form and shoved it across the desk to me.

"How much do you think I can get for all this?" I asked.

"About five thousand. And you'll be lucky to get it. People aren't interested in taking on old liabilities these days."

Five thousand dollars sounded like a fortune to me. It would mean security for Olivia, Ned and me for some time to come. So I took a deep breath and signed the contract. "You'll let me know when you have a buyer then, Mr. Dean."

"Yes, ma'am. I'll be sure and let you know."

So there it was. I would sell off half of my assets in order to keep the other half. My mother's words echoed in my ears. A loss is worse than a lack.

It wasn't a week before Mr. Dean called me to say he had a client interested in the whole package, willing to pay the asking price. Saddened that it was happening so quickly, I hesitated. But Mr. Dean came down the next day with a formal offer. I didn't read it all—real estate legal talk—but the bottom line, five thousand dollars and no questions asked was all I wanted to see. Still I resisted, hoping for some kind of miracle before the sale was final.

"I'll think about the offer, but I'm not promising anything," I told him.

"You have to act within thirty days or the offer becomes null and void."

"Only thirty days?"

"Yes, ma'am, but I'd do it quickly, before this offer slips through your fingers. There may not be another one."

I took the papers and laid them on a side table in the parlor, meaning to look them over carefully at my leisure. But I couldn't bring myself to look at them, read the description of what I was parting with. I needed someone to talk this over with, and I knew that Cousin Will was strongly in favor of selling. Someone else. Tess Gorman.

I often went calling on Tess to sit on her porch and look out over Roaring Run and talk about the old days. Getting up in years, Tess had her own burdens, but she kept to herself and did what she could, never asking for charity.

The raspberries were coming on, so I took my sunbonnet and a basket and Olivia and trekked over to get Tess at the little house. The three of us climbed the hillside toward the old children's cemetery, a sad little burying ground on top of the hill where children of the iron workers rested in overgrown brambly peace. The raspberries were ready in abundance and we picked, wending our way around the outside of the berry patch. No need to go deeper. The berries were luscious and profuse.

Olivia chattered away about her pony cart and how much fun it was to drive it down to the river, but it wasn't long before her interest lagged and she sat down in the grass, eating more berries than she'd picked.

"You know I've an offer to buy everything up Roaring Run except your house, the tenant house and the furnace," I told Tess.

"I figured it wouldn't be long before you'd sell something. I guess owning property ain't to your advantage any more."

"I don't want to sell at all, but this offer would make us comfortable for a while. I'd like not to have to worry about where the money will come from to pay the taxes."

Tess peered at me from under her sunbonnet. "So what's hindering you?"

"Oh, you know. All the memories, the history. Everything Mt. Etna used to be."

"Well, depending on who comes along, it could come back. You know, some folks like to fix up the old places and make them beautiful again."

"It'd have to be someone with a lot of money."

We stepped back from the berry bushes and sat down on a makeshift bench—nothing more than a log, really, by the cluster of sad little graves while Olivia walked among the tombstones, reading names and dates out loud, asking if I knew this one or that.

"They're from the mid-1800s, dear. How old do you think I am?"

The child thought a moment, then said, "Seventy."

I swatted at her with my apron. "You scamp! I'm barely thirty-one!"

Soon bored with the tombstones, she wandered off to pick wild flowers and Tess and I resumed our discussion.

"Even this, Tess." I nodded toward the cemetery, gravestones leaning askew. "I'd like to preserve even this. It meant something to someone long ago. I hate to let go of it."

"Hate to let go of the past, do you? There's more than a few would like to shake it off and never think about it again."

"I know. But if you've lived it—if it's a part of you, been fed to you with your mother's milk, it's hard to let it go."

Tess took her corncob pipe out of her apron pocket, tamped it down and lit it. I hoped Olivia wouldn't see her. I always thought she seemed common when she smoked that pipe. Well, I guess she was, but she was also kind and funny and wise. She sucked hard to get it started, then turned to me. "Keep your memories—can't nobody take that away—and let the rest go. It's still here for you to look at and remember. You don't have to own it to love it."

Good old sensible Tess knew how to get to the core of things. Selling didn't mean annihilation. The place would still be here. I could look at it, love it, remember it, without having to keep it all up. I smiled. "You always set me to rights, Tess. Bless you. I think I can let it go now."

I was hesitant to tell Richard about my intention to sell, for I knew it would hurt him to see any of it go, but we both knew the necessity of it.

Chapter 18

Richard, 1912

I was of the opinion that the only thing wanting at Mt. Etna was a husband for Sarah, but being given to shyness when it came to Sarah, I kept my peace and went on grinding flour. She relied on me for what was needed to keep Mt. Etna going, and I obliged, ever hopeful that she'd notice me in some way other than as a friend. After all, she was well past thirty and I was thirty-five. A man can't wait forever.

When Captain Andrew MacPhail returned for a month's leave from his long assignment in California, he found Mt. Etna changed in ways the rest of us had barely noticed.

"I see the canal basin is filling in and sprouting trees," he told me as we walked about on an inspection tour. "Not enough, though. You need to fill in those ditches so there isn't standing water for the mosquitoes to breed."

I nodded, knowing he was right, but sorry to lose what was left of the good skating ponds.

Andrew's experiences in the military had made him cautious about mosquito-borne plagues. Sarah pooh-poohed the idea. "We've lived with mosquitoes all our lives, Andrew. Never been sick yet."

"*Yet* being the operative word," he reproved, catching Olivia by both hands and swinging her around in a circle. The child was delighted with her status as a favorite niece.

Reunited once more, the three MacPhail children spent much time on the front porch reminiscing about their childhood. Having grown up there in concert with them, I was welcome to join in. But my memories were not as privileged as theirs, and when the subject of schooling came up I slipped into the background. I'd only made it through the eighth grade at Mt. Etna School, rarely left the village, and had seen nothing of the world, while Andrew loved to regale us with stories of far off places and wondrous cultures we could only imagine.

But Sarah was more concerned with Andrew's marital status than with his travels. "When will you marry, Andrew? You really must, you know. Else how will the MacPhail name be carried on?"

I could have reminded her that the blood line, if not the name, was thriving in Blair Four right now, but that would have been unkind.

"I've thought about it some, but Army life is hard on a woman. I've had my eye on one or two over the years, but nothing has come of it."

"I know! We should have Will introduce you to Altoona society. He and Beth know everybody. Maybe something could develop there."

Andrew laughed. "If I leave it to you, my fate'll be sealed for sure!"

"Well, leave it to me, then. I'll send a note to William this afternoon."

"I was thinking I'd ride down to Huntingdon and see if Bert Judge is open to the notion."

Sarah's eyebrows went up. So Andrew and Bert had kept up a correspondence over the years, and he was anxious to see her now. That threw Sarah into a bit of a tizzy. For some reason, she didn't care much for Bert and did her best to discourage the match, but Andrew paid no attention, and before we knew it, Bert was a daily visitor.

Brash and unconventional as before, Bert walked right into the MacPhail family and made herself at home. She struck up an instant friendship with Olivia, rechristened her Ollie and encouraged every sign of rebelliousness or questioning of convention that showed up in the child, adding to Sarah's list of reasons why Andrew shouldn't marry her.

One afternoon about a week into his visit, Andrew brought a new notion into our lives. "Know what you need around here, Sarah? A motor car."

"A motor car? Really? Glory, Andrew, what would I do with a motor car?"

"Learn to drive it and take yourself about. You live here in splendid isolation while the world marches on, my dear. The world marches on."

Sarah giggled out loud at the prospect of a motor car. Surely Andrew couldn't be serious. "Do you know how they work? Can you drive one?"

"Yes, I do, and I can. The Army keeps up with the times and expects its officers to do the same."

Sarah fell silent, thinking about the prospect. Andrew was right about our living in isolation. Some of the more prosperous farmers and town folk already had motor cars, and Sarah did like to think of herself as keeping up with the times. So before Andrew left, they took the shay to Hollidaysburg where Frank Thompson took orders for the Oldsmobile Curved Dash model, and within six weeks the car was theirs. This posed a small problem, however, for Andrew had gone to his next assignment and neither Ned nor Sarah knew how to drive the car. That was left to me, and while I was grateful not to have so much to do with horses on their account, I found the responsibility heavy.

Driving a motor car in those days was an iffy proposition, fraught with dangers and pitfalls unfamiliar to a miller's son from Roaring Run. There was the ever present danger of flat tires, oil leaks, running off the road, shying horses and chickens running and squawking in every direction. I don't know how many chickens I killed in that first year of driving—maybe a hundred, considering that some must have died of a heart attack and others were caught by a wily fox waiting in the roadside bushes for an hysterical hen to present herself for lunch.

In spite of Sarah's misgivings, Bert Judge became Andrew's bride-to-be. The Huntingdon beauty whose quotient of adventure made her the ideal mate for an Army officer hadn't been in a hurry to marry young. Her father had died and left her quite well fixed for both money and property so she'd spent several years doing exactly as she pleased. A modern women up for anything, capable of standing on her own two feet or on yours if you stood still for too long, Bert dressed in the newest style, long, simple lines and free flowing gowns, shortened skirts and even, on occasion, trousers!

She'd been sent off to Carlisle to a finishing school as a girl, then on to Juniata College, but little was said about her education. Some speculated that she'd spent more time smoking than studying. Sarah found her disconcerting, not at all the kind of woman she'd have chosen for a sister-in-law, or for a companion for Olivia, but there it was. Try as she might to discourage it, Olivia and Bert became fast friends. With or without Sarah's approval, Bert Judge heralded more change for Mt. Etna, ready or not.

Chapter 19

Ned, 1914

Sarah'd be mad at me if she knew I go over to Blair Four sometimes to hide out and watch Jacob. Marta's brother Josip got married and moved away to work in another quarry, but Andros stayed at Blair Four, married and had a bunch of kids, but he still kept Marta and Jacob with him. I didn't even get to see Jacob until he was four years old. Andros always kept a sharp eye on Marta, and when he was gone to work, his wife was always there, so Marta and I couldn't see each other.

Then once, when Jacob was four, I was out in the woods hunting when I heard talking and laughter over near our 'cabin'. I crept up through the woods and watched. There was Marta, with her sister-in-law and three little children, out gathering walnuts. One of the children was Jacob. I would have recognized him anywhere. His hair was dark, like Marta's and curly, like mine. His eyes were blue, also like mine, and he was a sturdy little chap, bright and curious. I stayed hidden and watched, listened, held captive by my son's beauty.

As I watched Andros's wife wander away in search of more walnuts, I saw my chance to speak to Marta.

"Marta." A loud whisper.

She sat up, alert, listening.

"Over here."

She looked around. I waved, then ducked down behind the logs. She rose and walked toward me, casual, eyes on the ground as though looking for walnuts. I held my breath, hoping to get maybe ten seconds with her.

"Jacob!" She called our son over and pretended to show him some walnuts on the ground near me. Dear Marta. I held my breath, took in my son in a long, hungry gaze. Marta smiled at me, looked around and stepped away as her sister-in-law wandered back.

I heard her say, "Let's go." to Marta, and Marta took Jacob's hand and led him away. I watched them disappear among the trees, the sound of my son's voice caressing my ears.

"Mama, can we stop and see if Bela is home?"

"No, Jacob. It's near supper time. Maybe tomorrow."

After that, I would find any way to see the boy, if only a glimpse of him at play in the school yard. It took another two years before I felt safe enough to station myself near Andros's house and watch, as I had in my youth—not from the limbs of a tree this time. I just walked past the house looking for even a glimpse of my son. Sometimes I put a little gift—a ball of string, a fish hook, one of my flies—under a rock beside a fence post, hoping Marta would see me put it there and lead Jacob to the discovery. After a few tries, he had the idea, so it became a regular routine. I think Andros knew I came around, but he pretended not to. Eventually I didn't have to hide—I just went over to watch Jacob and talk to Marta. She was still my friend and I told her all about Bert and Andrew and how much Sarah didn't like Bert, and how much Ollie did like her, and Marta would laugh at that.

Jacob was a fine little boy, real free and easy with people. He'd go right up and talk to anyone. I was glad for that. He didn't know I was his pa. Marta thought it best if he didn't know it, so I just visited once in a while. I'd bring him things I found in the woods, like acorns and walnuts, deer antlers or a bird's nest now and then. In the spring I'd take him fishing, show him where all the big ones hid out. Every time I saw him, I felt like crying. He was so beautiful and bright, and I wished I could be with him all the time.

I didn't let on that I still cared about Marta and Jacob because Sarah would have tried to keep me away from Blair Four. She'd get all wrought up when the subject even came up—like she was afraid I'd go over there and get in trouble again. I understood why she was afraid, even if I wasn't.

Sometimes I thought it was good for Sarah to get wrought up over something besides me, unless that something was Ollie. Ollie was funny and nice, and she and I had good times when Sarah wasn't around. Sarah was way too proper and she was getting worse as she got older. So I considered it a mission to make fun of her sometimes, and Ollie was always right there to appreciate it. It was a good day when I could get the better of Sarah. She had way too many opinions.

There was a war on way across the ocean and everybody was always talking about if we would get in it. Most people didn't want us to, but my brother Andrew thought it would be fine. He'd have to go, and he said it would 'further his military career,' whatever that meant. Sarah said boys from Mt. Etna, Blair Four, Carlim and Williamsburg would have to go and some of them would get killed. I didn't guess the Army would want me. I was almost thirty and everyone still thought I was slow so the Army would probably think that, too. Well, I was used to it and I liked Mt. Etna, so I didn't think I'd go.

Sometimes Richard would drive by where I was fishing in one of the runs, and he would always stop and talk to me. I liked that. I even told him about how I visited Marta and Jacob, and he said that was fine. I thought Richard Trethaway ought to get married to Sarah.

Sarah

Andrew and Bert have been married for three years now, and I must say life has been interesting since then. Andrew was assigned to a fort in New York after they married—Brooklyn, in fact, and as usual he bloomed and grew with the Army. Bert fit right in with the other Army wives—her penchant for adventure matching theirs. There was nothing she detested so much as a shrinking violet, and she mirrored Andrew's enthusiasm for life stride for stride. They'd probably stay in New York for quite some time unless that worrisome war in Europe reached our shores.

Ned had settled down quite nicely—seemed satisfied to stay home and live the quiet life. He tied his flies—I sold them locally—and fished to his heart's content. I didn't know what happened to that Marta girl or her child. Ever since that whole incident and Claire's death, I'd avoided Blair Four. Honestly, hardly a week went by that there wasn't some fight, stabbing or even murder over there. If it wasn't that, it was some poor soul getting blown to bits in an explosion or killed by flying rock. I don't know how those poor people managed to keep body and soul together, but it was none of my concern. I was kept busy enough raising Olivia, whose presence gave my life new meaning.

Olivia and Ned became close friends—did everything together—roamed the woods, hunted mushrooms, picked berries, shot squirrels, and fished, of course. Olivia found everything to do with Ned fascinating, and I was glad for that. I didn't know if Ned's thoughts ever strayed to that other child growing up in Blair Four—he would have been about seven—but he certainly seemed content with Olivia tagging after him as though he'd created the universe.

Nevertheless, it seemed as though there was always something to disturb the peace around here. Now it was Bert—Andrew's wife. Every summer she descended upon us, expecting accommodations of her own, access to the motor car and general freedom to roam about the countryside stirring things up. Bert was quite the suffragette, you see, and determined to make a pest of herself at political meetings, parading about carrying banners, posters, flags, whatever. Very outspoken, too, to anyone she met, as though people around here had any thoughts about women voting. I secretly wished she and Andrew would have children—thought that would give her something to think about besides her political views, but none arrived.

Bert gave Olivia a nickname—Ollie. I didn't like it; Olivia is a beautiful name, and feminine. But Bert would call her Ollie, and Ned picked it up—Richard, too, and Andrew when he visited. I was out numbered, but I persisted in calling her by her given name.

As soon as Bert and Andrew married I worried that Olivia would come under Bert's influence, and I was right to worry. I didn't know exactly what I was afraid of, but it didn't take long to show itself. Olivia observed and imitated every move Bert made and was keen to go where Bert went, say what Bert said, and take as gospel whatever Bert believed. I had a struggle on my hands just to keep Olivia on the right path.

Bert would come over to the manor house from her apartment in the tenant house across from the old store, dressed for riding or for driving, expecting Richard to be available at a snap of her fingers to provide whatever she fancied that day. He didn't seem to mind, either. In fact he seemed to like her quite some, and that did not set well with me, I can tell you. Richard was just a nice country boy, not used to the wiles of a woman like that, and I was afraid he'd succumb to her charms and develop a crush on her. To what end?

I warned him of her more than once. "Now, Richard, you don't have to do her bidding unless you want to. You have plenty of work to do around here as it is. You don't need to cater to Bert's every whim."

He smiled. "That's okay, Sarah. I get a kick out of her. She's got spunk, that one."

"Spunk that might lead her *and* my brother to disaster. She's way too modern for folks around here."

"Is that you talking, or have you heard something?"

I sniffed. "Nothing specific, but I know what these ladies will be saying behind their fans. Believe me, Richard, Bert's reputation will suffer if she keeps on acting like some kind of socialite. Folks will put her in her place."

Richard gave me a doubtful smile and went out to crank up the car for Bert. I felt mean for my criticism, but try as I would not to show it, just doing my work and minding my own business, it came out anyway.

Chapter 20

Sarah, 1914

Just yesterday we had a little set-to about Bert's sense of entitlement. I was helping Mrs. Beck can tomatoes when Bert sent Buddy Walsh over. "Sarah, could you get Richard to bring up the car? Miss Bert has to run up to Hollidaysburg for a meeting."

"Why, I guess you can ask him, but Richard's liable to be busy. Why doesn't she just come start it up herself?" I let a tone of doubt creep into my voice hoping the boy would let Bert know it wasn't entirely suitable for her to think Richard should be at her beck and call.

"Hollidaysburg? Can I go, Mama Sarah?" That was Olivia, hoping to join Bert at some crusading ladies' meeting.

"I should say not. I won't have you running around after Bert stirring people up about getting the vote for women."

"Why not?"

"Because it's a silly, frivolous cause, and hopeless."

Olivia stood on one foot, arms outstretched, balancing. "Why silly?"

"Because men are never going to let us have the vote. They'd be giving up their power over us."

"Why should they have power over us?"

Her questions were getting under my skin. "I'm not saying they should, just that they do. It's always been that way. Get used to it."

"But Bert says we can change it if we all work together and make enough of a nuisance of ourselves so that the men get tired of saying no and just say yes."

I sighed and handed her a towel to wipe the dishes with. "If it were only that easy."

Within a half hour, Bert entered the kitchen. "If it's a problem for Richard to start up the car, I guess I can give it a try." Her voice betrayed her irritation.

She'd been raised to think she was entitled and being the wife of a West Point officer reinforced that. That might have worked on an Army post in New York, but in Mt. Etna, it surely caused more consternation than admiration.

"I'm sure you can handle it." I said it without looking at her, sure she'd get my message, however mildly put.

"Bet I could do it," Olivia said, giving Bert a hello hug.

"No doubt you could, my dear." She returned the hug and held Olivia at arm's length to study her outfit. "Are you ready?"

"Ready?" I asked. "Ready for what?"

"For her first suffragette meeting." Bert beamed as Olivia hopped up and down, clapping her hands in glee.

"This is the first *I've* heard about it. I'd think you'd ask before assuming it was all right."

Ignoring my reprove, Bert stepped out on the porch and called for Buddy who was still playing along the canal bank. "Buddy! Go fetch Mr. Trethaway. Tell him he's needed now at the manor house. Hurry on, please."

Richard obliged within ten minutes to start the car for her, and Bert gave him a flirtatious smile and a toss of her head before blithely climbing into the driver's seat for the trip to Hollidaysburg, Olivia at her side.

I had to admit that deep down I envied Bert's rash confidence and sense of adventure. If there wasn't something exciting afoot, she'd stir something up. Andrew seemed to delight in her independence and brash disregard for all convention, and, always having a special place in my heart for Andrew, I secretly wished I could be that kind of girl. I wasn't ready to let Olivia go down that path, but I could see that preventing it would require a strong and public stand against it. Knowing how Olivia would react to such a stand gave the victory over to Bert without a fight.

Bert didn't always attend church when she was visiting, and that bothered me because, of course, Olivia saw that as exciting and liberating. One Sunday morning not three weeks into Bert's summer visit, Olivia asked to stay home from church. Of course I insisted that she go, and spent the rest of the morning in the company of a sulking nine-year-old.

The next evening when Bert and Olivia got back from a drive to God knew where, Bert stopped and left the car for Richard to put away. "Whew, that was a busy day," she said.

"Really? Where did you go?"

"Hollidaysburg. To a meeting of the Women's Suffrage Society at the Presbyterian Church. They're quite a fine group. Full of hard-headed determination to get the vote for women. You should join us, Sarah. You'd meet some interesting women and work for a worthy cause."

"Sounds like a fool's errand to me."

"Why?"

"We both know the men aren't going to give us the vote. Why should they? And why should we sacrifice our dignity to a lost cause?"

"Lost cause? Oh, my dear, it *will* come. Mark my words. Women will get the vote, nationwide, before long."

Olivia chimed in. "Yes, Mama Sarah, they will, but it'll take a lot of hard work and dedication to make that happen." Spoken like a thoroughly indoctrinated child.

"What makes you so sure?" I asked Bert.

"Why the women I meet all around who are intent on suffrage," Bert responded. "They're well organized and determined. The Hollidaysburg group had a booth at the county fair last week and collected $50 in donations. They garner more support for the cause every day, much of it from men."

The cause. Really. I felt disinclined to argue with her, but in my mind, Bert was headed for grave disappointment and taking Olivia with her. Sometimes I wished Andrew wouldn't send her to spend summers with us, but I thought maybe he needed a break from her constant high energy. Bert's antics strained my relations with the local folk. I saw them snickering behind their hands and felt as though I—and, of course, Olivia—was being judged on her behalf.

Each summer she came back with as much sauce as ever and involved herself more deeply in the local suffragette movement, fanning the flames with new ideas from New York and urging the local chapters into more defiance and vocalization. After that first meeting, Olivia was at her side for the duration of the struggle, mimicking her every move and parroting her every phrase.

Andrew rarely came with Bert, and if he did, he stayed only for a few days, preferring, I thought, the company of his fellow soldiers to that of his wife. Even so, when they were together, Andrew and Bert seemed to love and find delight in one another. Andrew said over and over how he wanted his children to grow up in the Juniata Valley as he had, surrounded by the love and heritage of family, so of course I felt obliged to put up with Bert's impertinence for his sake. But those elusive children made me wonder the why of it. Was she barren or just deliberately avoiding motherhood?

Ned seemed to like Bert as much as Richard did, even though it took him a while to get used to her brash manner. She took to him right away and encouraged his bad habits, like smoking cigars and drinking beer. She would even drink beer with him! Not a dainty glass of claret like a lady, mind you, but beer—from a bottle! Like a common trollop. And she never even noticed when he swore in front of her. Never winced. Never asked him to watch his language. Words like hell and damn became common, until Olivia began using them, and I'd had enough.

"Ned! You must stop using foul language in front of Olivia. She'll be talking like that before you know it—like those uncouth little urchins over at Blair Four."

Ned started at that. He never talked about the one little urchin he'd sired, but I saw a flash of hurt pass behind his eyes. "All right, Sarah. I'll watch it."

But, of course, Bert sidled up to him and put her arm around him and said, "Don't give it a thought, Ned. They probably hear worse than that at school." And pecked him on the cheek. Just what I needed, an alliance between Bert and Ned.

And, to make matters worse, it wasn't a week before I heard that word, Hell, come out of his mouth again, and right in front of Olivia. It seemed to me that things just weren't the way they used to be and that Ned, Bert and Olivia were allied in favor of that.

I appealed to Richard, but his head had already been turned. "She's not so bad," he told me. "Just a little head strong. Take a helluva man to keep up with her."

"Richard, I would prefer that you not use that kind of language in my presence."

"Yes, ma'am."

Chapter 21

Richard, 1915

Remember when I said nothing ever changed around Mt. Etna? Well, things changed all right. Slowly and in subtle ways, but they changed. Sarah got a bee in her bonnet over Andrew's wife. Too much change for one so used to having things pretty much her own way. New winds blowin'—and Sarah was determined to stand against them, whether or no. I could see both sides—Sarah clinging to the way things had always been, and Miss Bert bent on loosening them up a bit. It would have been fun to watch if I didn't have an interest in it, but I didn't want Sarah thinking I'd gone over to Bert, or Bert getting it in her head that I was stuck on Sarah.

Ned was happy, though. Always did favor anything that challenged Sarah's authority. Good for him to get over himself a little, and Bert was just the woman for that. She even taught him to drive. Yep. If Sarah knew, she'd have gone into apoplexy. Give Ned more independence so he could run about the country getting more young ladies in the family way? No, I didn't think he'd ever go that way again, but Sarah would worry over it for sure.

I was hesitant to teach Ned to drive because I wasn't sure he'd be any good at it. He tended to be a bit clumsy, and I was afraid steering might be hard for him, so I just let it ride for a while. But he was fascinated with that Oldsmobile, and the next thing I knew Bert took on the task of teaching him.

I figured to mind my own business and let Sarah handle it once she found out, but Bert was way ahead of me. Instead of telling Ned he wouldn't be good at it, she encouraged him. I guess she figured it was a painless way to let him see for himself how hard it would be. So she got me to get the car out for her and drove down the road a piece where Ned was waiting and she showed him how the pedals and steering worked and next thing, she moved over and let him drive.

Well, that was an adventure, according to how Bert told it the next day. They drove down along the river and up over the hill to Fox Hollow. Ned jerked and jumped the car and stalled it and swerved from left to right and right to left. Bert had to hold on with both hands, and she still got jolted almost out of the car. They turned down toward the railroad where Fox Run winds through the underpass toward the track that leads to Blair Four when the car stalled right in the waters of Fox Run.

Bert got out and tried to crank it again, but it wouldn't turn over. There it sat blocking the underpass when a truck and a wagon came along waiting to go through. The two drivers got out and tried to start the car, but it was useless. Finally they pushed it out of the underpass on the Fox Hollow side and let it sit.

Bert and Ned sat there for the better part of an hour waiting to see if it would start, but then they gave up and walked home, leaving the car sitting by the underpass. They came to get me, and the three of us walked back to see what we could do. Now I'm not mechanically inclined, so I barely figured out how to drive that jitney, let alone fix it. But I looked it over as best I could. Couldn't figure out what was wrong, so we trekked back to

Mt. Etna, aware that now we had a problem. Sarah was bound to notice the car was gone and want to know what had happened to it.

It wasn't long in coming. The next morning, Sarah sent word by young Ollie that she wanted to see me, so I walked back to the manor house. Sarah said she wanted to go to the cemetery over on the hill above Fox Hollow to plant flowers on the family graves for Decoration Day which was coming up. I suggested she take her flowers and watering can and trowel in the wagon. Even offered to hitch up the horse and drive her over. That was all right with her, and she waited while I got the wagon ready and loaded her flowers and stuff in it. Then she called Ollie who pulled herself up into the back of the wagon and we were off to the cemetery.

As we passed the turn to Blair Four Sarah looked down toward the underpass. "Wait, Richard. Is that my car sitting down there? How'd it get there?"

"Well, ma'am, I think Bert took it out for a drive yesterday and had some trouble with it. I went to look at it, but I couldn't get it started, either."

"Well, what are we going to do? Let it sit there 'til it rusts? Drive down and let's see if we can get it started."

I was pretty sure we couldn't, and there was nobody else around that knew enough about cars to fix them, so I figured to go to Hollidaysburg and get somebody to come down and look at it. But Sarah was adamant, so I turned the wagon down the track to the underpass where a swarthy-looking man was sitting on the running board with a wooden box beside him. He stood up, smiled, and waved as we drove up.

"Good day. Your car?" he asked.

"Yes, it's mine," Sarah replied. "What are you doing with it?"

"Nothing. Fine car. Just looking at." He tucked his wooden box under one arm and stood by the car, cap in his hands. "Why you leave here over night?"

I got down from the wagon and went over to the car. "Broke down. Yesterday. Don't know how to fix it."

The man put the box down and smiled. "Let me look? I know cars. I can fix."

"Sure. I'd be glad for the help."

"Now, Richard," Sarah admonished. "We don't know him."

Her built-in distrust of anyone from Blair Four embarrassed me. The man looked all right. Tall, dark haired, clean shaven—unlike most of the quarry workers who all sported various kinds of moustaches. He had the look of a foreigner about him—ill-fitting clothes and short on English, but he didn't look like a quarry worker, so I asked.

"You from Blair Four? Work in the quarry?"

"No. Piano tuner. Travel around. Tune pianos."

That reassured Sarah. "Oh, we have a piano that needs tuning. You could come do it for us."

The man took off his jacket and lifted the hood of the car. He was soon busy tinkering with this and that, and before long, he straightened up and turned to me. "Crank her up."

I bent to the crank as he pressed the starter and the car roared to life. "That's great. Thank you. Where did you learn so much about cars?"

"I have one back home in Budapest. I drive it around some." He was an engaging fellow, all smiles and friendly. We thanked him again and invited him to Mt. Etna to tune the big piano in the front parlor that afternoon. As we left him standing by the car, holding his wooden box, it occurred to me that he could drive the car to Mt. Etna and wait for us there, but Sarah was having none of that.

"You're too trusting, Richard. He could just drive away with the car and that'd be the last we'd see of him."

"Well, yes, he could, but I don't think he would."

I clucked to the horse and turned the wagon back toward the main road up through Fox Hollow to the cemetery. The work there took us the rest of the morning, so by the time we got back to Mt. Etna, we were ready for lunch. As we drove up, there in the front yard stood the Oldsmobile, shining clean from just being washed.

"Looks like our friend took it upon himself to deliver the car—and wash it, too," I observed.

Sarah didn't say anything; she just got down from the wagon and headed for the front door. The stranger stood smiling by the auto, nodding to her as she passed. I followed her into the house, hoping she would at least invite him to lunch.

"I think he's impertinent. Taking it upon himself to drive the car home. Washing it was just a ploy to get a tip. I'm not comfortable with foreigners. You know that." Sarah tended to get huffy when challenged.

"We don't have to ask him to move in. We could just give him lunch, let him tune the piano and send him on his way. I'll stick around and keep an eye on him if you want."

"That won't be necessary. Ned is here, and Olivia can come get you if need be."

There went my lunch invitation. Oh, well, I still had flour to sack. I excused myself and unhitched the wagon. The gentleman was sitting on the front porch now, talking to Ollie. It looked safe enough to me, so I took my leave.

By the time I returned a few hours later, the piano had been tuned, the auto garaged and a broken window pane in the carriage house replaced. Sarah and Alex—Alessandro Bodnar, officially—were sitting on the front porch sipping tea and laughing at the antics of Ollie trying to demonstrate her prowess as a gymnast on the lawn.

"Richard! Come up. I've just been getting to know Alex. You won't believe this, but he was a concert pianist in Hungary!"

"I knew those hands didn't belong to a quarry worker," I observed, taking a seat beside our new friend. Long tapered callous-free fingers, and neat, clean finger nails. No quarryman, he.

Alex was soon engaged to tune up the organ at the church on the hill above Fox Hollow, and when finished he treated us to a concert, the likes of which had never been put through that old pump organ. All I'd ever heard from it were slow, mournful dirges on a Sunday morning, but Alex made it sing and dance, like a babbling brook. His lilting tune made Ollie rise from her pew and clog dance in the aisle, ignoring reminders from Sarah that this was a place of worship.

"Let her dance," Alex said. "Surely God loves dancing, else why did he give us music?"

Sarah smiled and said no more. She was already enthralled.

Chapter 22

Sarah, 1916

It seems I'd let myself fall in love again in spite of my best efforts to avoid it. And with a foreigner, of all people! Alex Bodnar came to us early in the summer, and quickly warmed his way into my heart. I felt so foolish—at my age—even thinking about a man. But this one was so special. A concert pianist, composer and conductor! Now reduced to an itinerant piano tuner. So sad. He belonged in New York or London, plying his trade. I remember the afternoon when all of this came tumbling out of him, so humble, so unprepossessing. Ned had taken Olivia berry picking, and Alex had just finished repairing the broken leg of a side table, when, as I thanked him profusely as usual, he held up a hand.

"No need to thank me. You've been so kind. To give me a place to stay and work to do. It is I who thank you."

"Just one of the workers' cabins. Certainly no palace, Alex. You deserve more."

"That is all behind me now, Sarah. I left it all when I chose to leave Hungary rather than fight for the Austrian Army in this hellish war."

It was truly a hellish war, had been from the start, and all reports out of Europe were that it was a hopeless stalemate, doomed to drag on forever. I feared for Andrew that the United States might yet be drawn in, but knew it was beyond my power to influence.

"You made the right choice, even though you had to leave so much behind. Don't you think you could pick up where you left off and become a pianist here?"

He shook his head. "I don't know anybody. The language is a problem. Besides, there are many musicians as talented as I. I'm just grateful to be here in a free country."

I understood that, but I still thought his talent was too great to be hidden in the woods. I didn't know anyone either, but I knew that given the right connections, Alessandro Bodnar would become famous again.

In the meantime he now lived with us, handyman, piano tuner, music teacher and tutor. Pleased to be the recipient of his help and talent, I slowly let him into my life. Everyone here— Olivia, Ned, Bert, even Richard seemed to like and respect Alex, accept him as a valued part of the community—at first. I think Richard might have had his doubts, but he kept his concerns to himself, noting that Alex and I were special friends.

I thought back to my days at Juniata College, wishing I'd kept up relationships so that I could call on influential people to give Alex the new start he needed. I thought perhaps Will and Aunt Beth would know someone who could offer a hand up, but both were getting up in years and out of the main stream, so little help there.

Alex was so good with Olivia. He taught her to play the piano, even sent to a mail order house for a book of Strauss Waltzes for her to play. Where he got the money, I didn't know, but there was no question that he would pay for it. The child became quite proficient on the piano, her fingers poised just right above the keys, her brow furrowed with intent. It was a joy to see her so engaged.

As for me, I felt myself falling in love from the start even though I'd made a conscious resolution not to let that happen. Besides, my former attitude about foreigners stood in stark contrast to this man, exceptional in every way, a dazzling, brilliant, talent, dropped in my lap by fate and destined to rule my very being. At forty, he'd already been well established in the Hungarian musical world, so his ambition, though real, wasn't as deep and gnawing as that of a younger man. He often said he'd be happy to stay in Mt. Etna and take care of us for the rest of his life rather than go back to his former life in Hungary.

We didn't rush into things, mind. We moved slowly toward one another, day by day learning more and wanting more. I'd long since given up any hope of love in my life, so perhaps that is why this was so delicious when it came. He stayed for the first week in a room in one of the old dormitories turned boarding house run by Mrs. Peight, but he soon fixed up one of the dilapidated workers' cabins for himself. His knowledge of things mechanical seemed endless, and he set himself to fixing anything that was broken in payment for his rent. I knew Richard was relieved to have such expert help—not to have all of the repairs and maintenance on his shoulders. After a few months Alex turned to restoring the manor house to its former glory, never asking for pay, just delighting in the chance to use his skills and appreciative of the fine design and structure of the old house.

Bert found him mildly interesting. Not as stimulating or given to bad habits as she would have liked, but she had to respect his skill and talent. She enlisted his help in keeping the

Oldsmobile running and sometimes asked him to give a little concert in support of her suffragette group. He did so obligingly, never asking for or accepting compensation. On these occasions Olivia was delighted to attend the concert and bask in Alex's reflected glory.

By now all the world was thinking this man was too good to be true. Well, indeed, he was. Kind, talented, intelligent, skilled, loving. I couldn't believe my good luck in finding him, even though as time passed and my infatuation became common knowledge, Bert and Richard allied in skepticism against him. I tried to hold my feelings in check, but Olivia and I were completely captivated so we became a house divided Bert and Richard against Olivia and me. Ned preferred to remain neutral. It was the single sad aspect of Alex's coming. Two camps, divergent in their opinions of him.

Alex made no assumption of affection, was a perfect gentleman at all times, and took no liberties. In fact, I was beginning to wonder if there were, perhaps, a wife or sweetheart back in Budapest, a possibility that Bert found interesting, but which Alex strongly denied. Finally, after tantalizing me for the whole summer and into the fall, one October evening he ventured to hold my hand as we walked along the old canal tow path through fallen leaves crackling under foot.

"Sarah," he began, "I've come to care a great deal for you."

"And I for you," I responded, my heart beating fast.

"I was hoping you would say that. I know I have little to offer, but I wonder if you would consider me a worthy candidate for your hand."

It was sudden, I know, but I'd been wishing for it, wanting it for so long, I was eager to assent. "Oh, Alex, yes! Yes, of course. I'm honored that you would even consider me."

"As am I."

So began our betrothal, the first for me, but, as I was to learn along the way, not the first for him. Not nearly. Alex had been quite the swain in Hungary, handsome, talented, rich. Women threw themselves at him, crowding backstage after every concert, soliciting his attention on the flimsiest of causes. He'd never married, but in a soul-baring session soon after his proposal, he revealed his many romances, anxious for me to know all about him so that he could be assured that I would love him no matter what. I did. No matter what.

Ned

I always knew Sarah longed for love. That's what made her so sour a lot of the time. So when Alex came along, I thought it might be fine, because she got real nice and smiled a lot more. Alex was always good to us. He fixed things and taught Ollie to make music and he even tried to teach me to play the piano. He said people like me were sometimes very good musicians, but I wasn't, and I didn't know what he meant by 'people like me.' Still, I thought he was all right if Sarah liked him, and she did.

It made Richard uneasy at first, then just sad. He should have married her when he had the chance. I told him to, but he didn't listen. Bert was the one that really wasn't sure about Alex. She said she liked him, but she didn't hang around much where he was. She'd get him to fix the car or to do odd jobs for her, but she never got silly or rowdy with him like she always did with me and Richard.

I asked her one day why she didn't like him.

"It's not that I don't like him. I just wonder about him, is all. We don't really know anything about him now, do we? What if he isn't who he says he is? What if he just thinks Sarah's rich and wants to get at her money?"

That got me worried. I hadn't thought of it, but Bert might be right. What if Alex didn't love Sarah at all, but wanted to marry her so he could be rich? Well, if Sarah thought he *did* love her, I guessed it would be all right as long as he never told her he didn't, and maybe he could get to love her if they got married. But what would he think if he found out we weren't really rich? What if he knew we'd already sold off a lot of what we had? It was puzzling.

When Bert told Andrew about Sarah wanting to marry Alex, he came right down from New York in a huff and told her she was being foolish. Of course Sarah didn't want to hear that. She shouted at Andrew and ran off to her room. That made me scared—made me want to noddle. I hadn't felt that way in such a long time, but hearing my brother and sister fight was upsetting. I went out and walked down the road to Richard's house. He was carrying in a load of firewood, so I helped him.

"What's on yer mind, Ned?"

"Andrew and Sarah are fighting."

"What about?"

"Alex."

"Oh, I see. Well, don't worry. It'll blow over."

"I don't know. They were yelling real loud, and Sarah was crying, too."

"I'd go over and see what's brewing, but I think we should just give them time to sort this out."

I didn't want to wait. I wanted it to stop. "Why doesn't Andrew like Alex? He's nice."

"I guess he's afraid Alex isn't who he says he is. He doesn't want Sarah to get hurt."

"Why doesn't he just write to somebody in Hungary and ask about Alex? Or go there and see?"

"There's a war on there, or near there, so it wouldn't be good to go now. But maybe he could write to somebody if he knew who to write to."

So there we were. We didn't know if Alex was who he said he was, and we didn't know anyone to ask. But I said, "If he's nice and does good work for us and he likes Sarah and she likes him, what's so bad about that? Even if we don't know all about him. I think you should judge people on how they are to you, not what other people think of them."

Richard seemed tired of talking about Sarah and Alex, so I told him I'd be going. He gave me a half-hearted wave and I left. I walked down Roaring Run Hollow past the little house, standing lonely in the moonlight. From the shadows in front of her porch, Tess Gorman called to me.

"That you, Ned? Whatcha doin' out all alone in the dark?"

"Just walking, Tess. I was up to see Richard."

I stepped closer, trying to make out her face in the dark.

"I hear they're fightin' over to the manor house. What're they so bullied up about?"

Tess was an old lady—somewhere in her seventies—and she'd lived at Mt. Etna most of her life. There was a story about her mysterious husband that went off south at the end of the War Between the States and never came back. My papa always said he had respect for Tess, so I did, too.

"Sarah wants to marry Alex, but everybody's against it, 'cause they say they don't know if Alex is who he says he is."

"Who else would he be? A penniless immigrant with nothing? That's what he says he is. Might have been a famous musician once, but he ain't that now, so what are they so worried about?"

"I don't know. They get all wrought up over things I don't understand. If Sarah wants to marry him, it should be her business."

"Right, Ned. You tell 'em. Sometimes I think the MacPhails put on airs like they're so great. I remember the good old days when they *was* rich, but they *ain't* rich no more, so why worry? Tell Sarah to come see me. I'll tell her a thing or two."

So I went back home feeling like it was Sarah's life and her decision, so Andrew could just butt out.

They finally stopped yelling at each other and sat down to talk. I listened at the door because they always sent me out when they talked.

Andrew said, "I can't really stop you from marrying who you please, but I want to see something left of the iron plantation. After all, it's been in our family for generations, and I hope some day my children will still have it after I'm gone. Ned won't ever have any children, and you probably wouldn't either, so that's why I'm concerned. I wanted my children to be the heirs, and I don't want you to marry in haste."

That all sounded smart except for one thing. Andrew didn't have any children either and it didn't look like he was about to get any.

Sarah sighed. "All right. Alex and I will wait a while, but I'm sure he's a good man, and I intend to marry him some day."

Alex wasn't there for this discussion. He was back in his workers' cabin waiting for it to be over. I felt sorry for him. It hurts when people don't like you.

The next morning I was just getting out of bed when I heard the whistle for the 6:30 express to Harrisburg and Philadelphia. I looked out the window and saw Alex standing by the depot, his wooden box of piano tuning tools under his arm. I opened the window and shouted at him to come back, but the train was too loud and he didn't hear me. I saw him get on the train, turn to look toward the manor house, and wave. I don't think he heard me or saw me. I think he was waving good-bye to Sarah.

That day, Andrew and I walked around the place and I showed Andrew all the things Alex had fixed and made better. "I wished he'd stayed, because he really made Sarah better, but I knew he couldn't stay where people didn't like him."

"Well, Ned, you don't understand everything. Sometimes you have to leave it to Sarah and me to decide what's best."

Right then I started to wonder if I liked Andrew or Bert—or even Richard—'cause they made Sarah and Alex so sad.

Chapter 23

Sarah, 1918

Now we went and got ourselves involved in Europe's war, and Andrew's been sent to France. He brought Bert down from New York early last August, and left her here for the duration of the war. He actually seemed quite excited to go. I was deeply concerned about him, but Bert seemed to take the whole thing in stride. I didn't know how she'd get along staying at Mt. Etna full time, but I needn't have worried. She made allies of Ned and Richard and, indeed, anyone else who liked to play cards, drink beer, smoke and swear. They would go to the tenant house of an evening, rowdy, boisterous and unrestrained. I kept Olivia as far away as possible from their influence, but she *would* go over there every time my back was turned.

Everything was tossed up in a basket around Mt. Etna. Bert took over the tenant house as usual, but it needed repair if it was to be used year round, and Richard had enough to do at the mill and helping me run this place. He had Ned for an apprentice, but Ned would just as soon fish as breathe, so it mostly fell to Richard. Made me angry all over again to think of how they ran poor Alex off. He'd have been a great help in those days.

1918 started out with a January blizzard that harkened all the old timers back to the winters of the 1800s. I didn't remember anything this cold and windy with the snow piled up so high if folks opened their doors an avalanche would fall in. We stayed inside for a week while Richard, bless him, carried wood and water to keep us comfortable. I invited Bert to stay with us so Richard would have only one abode to tend to. I don't know what we'd have done without him. Ned would have had to step up, but I still didn't know how high Ned could step.

Olivia was delighted to have Bert so close. They spent every evening together, doing puzzles, playing the piano, singing those new, popular songs and playing parlor games like Flinch. Those games often got so boisterous and competitive I didn't think them seemly for a young girl to be playing, but as usual, I was voted down, two to one.

Andrew hadn't seen much action by then, but he wrote that it was coming. We could bet on that. You'd think Bert would be in tears over his being in danger, but she was sunny as ever and full of talk about how close women were to getting the vote. She even tried to enlist my help in the cause again, and, smarting over her strong influence on Olivia, I agreed to attend a meeting, sure I wasn't going to like it.

The day we went to Hollidaysburg for the meeting was wet and rainy, leaving us sodden and dripping by the time we arrived. I stayed in the background as Bert and Olivia greeted friends and talked of future plans. Once the meeting began, I found myself interested in the talk if not enthusiastic about the chances of victory.

The meeting was followed by a luncheon where people were assigned seats at various tables, a deliberate ploy to encourage mixing. My tablemates, Mrs. Johnson, Mrs. Bryson and Mrs. Polk were friendly and welcoming, and I soon realized I had more in common with them than I thought. It was a pleasant interlude that helped me see what motivated Bert, and through her, Olivia.

"Did you enjoy the meeting, Mama Sarah?" Olivia wanted to know on the drive home.

"Yes, dear. I did. The ladies were all very kind and welcoming."

"Yes, but did you find the discussion inspiring?"

"Well, yes, somewhat."

"Somewhat? How can you say just somewhat? This is a cause for all of us."

"I straightened my self in the car seat, Bert intent behind the wheel. "Olivia, you are young and impressionable. I find the whole movement capricious. I've lived long enough to know that these things aren't ever as wonderful as they're made out to be."

"But Mama Sarah, how can giving women the right to vote—to have a say—not be wonderful? We've lived long enough powerless under the yoke of man."

I sniffed at that. "That kind of thinking wasn't going to get you a husband when you grow up." I wanted to chide her more, turn her head in the other direction, pull her out from under Bert's sway before it was too late.

She shook her head. "No, ma'am. I wouldn't want the kind of husband who'd be opposed to women voting. Or anything else they wanted, for that matter."

It passed through my mind that she wouldn't have wanted to marry her own father, for sure. Phillip Chamberlain used and abused women. Maybe the fact that his daughter wouldn't put up with someone like him indicated real progress for women. I almost wished he could see her, know her now. I smiled.

Ned was delighted to have Bert here all the time as their friendship developed into a subtle three-way alliance against me. I wished Bert would see how hard it'd been for me to bring both Ned and Olivia along and support my efforts. It seemed her only purpose was to lead them into mischief, and Ned and Olivia were willing accomplices.

I heard from Alex about once a week, letters of encouragement and triumph. He'd fallen in with the musical intelligentsia of Philadelphia and earned a place with the symphony orchestra. He wasn't recognized for his individual talent at the piano just yet, but I was sure that would come in time. He continued to declare his love for me and his intention to return to Mt. Etna financially stable so the family couldn't assume he was after my money. I could have reassured them on my own, for there *was* no money. Not anymore, and I told Alex that before he left.

In the meantime, life was a jumble of trying to get Bert settled, get Olivia ready to attend high school in Williamsburg, keep up with maintenance all around the estate and keep the finances in good stead. I didn't get any help from anybody but Richard. Bert was too taken up with her suffrage crusade, Ned was Ned, and that left me to handle it all, so I really did appreciate Richard.

I knew it vexed him to know I still heard from Alex, but what could I do? One can't just turn love on or off like a faucet. I still hoped and believed that Alex and I would marry some day, with or without Richard's approval.

Some days I got so exhausted with carrying the load, I just wanted to give up. That's when I'd arrange a visit with Tess. She was such a good friend to my mother, and continued to be for me. Good old Tess. Cousin Will still maintained he should have married her when they were young, even though she was six years his senior. He said she was the most solid, level-headed woman he'd ever known, and he'd known her for the better part of seventy years.

So one spring morning I sent young Buddy over with a note, inviting Tess for tea and cakes. She arrived on foot, even though I would have sent a wagon for her.

"Well, now, what's on *your* mind? I know you didn't invite me just to chew the fat, so what is it?" Always direct, Tess didn't know how to couch her opinions in niceties.

"Oh, Tess, I'm just overwhelmed with all the work around here. I feel like the place is falling down with no hope to stop it. Richard tries to help, but he has the mill to look after, and no one else seems to give a damn."

"Harsh language from you, my dear. My advice would be to stop holding Richard off at arm's length and marry him. Close the mill down and let him take over managing the whole place. He's a good man and wanted you for his whole life."

"Oh, Tess, you don't understand. Alex isn't gone from my life. He's just gone for a while to make a career for himself, and when he comes back we'll get married."

Tess sat studying me for a long time. "You really believe that, don't you? It appears to me that if he was going to marry you, he could have done it already. He went away because he found this place too harsh and judgmental. What's changed there? Even with Andrew in France, he'd still have to face scrutiny."

"But he writes that he's got a place with the symphony orchestra and hopes to get an opportunity for a concert soon."

"I don't care what he writes or what he's told you. All you have to measure him by is what he *does,* and what he's *done* was to leave you. If he wants you so badly, why doesn't he send for you?"

"Oh, he couldn't do that. He isn't financially stable yet, and he knows I can't leave Mt., Etna."

Tess sniffed and took a sip of tea. "I think you're overlooking a fine man for a fantasy. Richard would lie down on the tracks for you. That other one left. That's all I say."

"I know what everyone thinks about Alex. I've had those thoughts myself, but deep down I still want to believe in him. I haven't forgotten that other time, when I was young and naïve at Juniata College. Don't you think I'm aware that such a thing could happen again?"

"All the more reason to protect yourself. Believe me, I know what it is to fall in love with the wrong man. Before you were even thought of, I fell in love with your uncle Robert. Everyone told me it was folly, but I couldn't hear them until it was too late. Then I found out they were right. All I want to do is keep you from going down that same path."

I reached out and patted her hand. "Thank you, Tess, for caring. I may make a colossal fool of myself again, but I can't bring myself to give up on Alex. He's such a fine man. The only reason you don't think so is that you don't know him."

After that encounter, I left Tess to her opinions and worked my way through the spring, struggling to keep all my responsibilities aloft, something like twirling plates on long sticks like I saw at a circus once. I comforted myself with Alex's letters, which continued to tell of wonderful strides for him, but, to my grave disappointment, seemed to push our future farther away. I tried not to notice—tried to keep up my optimism—but as the space between his letters widened, I longed for someone to talk to—someone who would tell me everything would be all right. There was no one. Bert had nothing good to say about Alex and counseled me to forget him. Olivia and Ned still liked him, but their approval carried no weight, and I wouldn't even broach the subject in a letter to Andrew.

August brought long and hot summer days. The temperature went well above a hundred degrees, making a swim in the river seem attractive, except for the fact that our dear old Juniata had become polluted with waste from the paper mill in Williamsburg. It brought economic good times to the little town, but those of us down river felt the other edge of the blade when our river turned brown, the rocks slimy and the fish dead. What a change from the days of my youth when we swam and played, fished and explored all along the river's length, taking its delights for granted.

In September, we heard the first rumors of influenza, called the Spanish Flu, breaking out in the trenches of France. At first it didn't seem that it could ever be as dangerous as the fighting itself, but we were to learn the irrationality of that belief. The numbers coming out of France were astonishing, but the fear really took hold of us when cases began appearing in the stateside Army camps and quickly spread to the civilian population.

Our fears for Andrew grew with the probability that he would be exposed and sickened, but we kept the thought of death at bay, heartened by hope that the war was winding down and that Andrew's strong constitution would be enough to defeat the flu. But October brought the dread news. Our brother, Major Andrew Curtin MacPhail, died of the flu on September 29, 1918 at a place called the Gondrecourt, France. To intensify our grief, he was buried in France in an American cemetery, never to return to his beloved Mt. Etna.

Bereft of her proud officer husband, Bert threw herself into fighting the flu here at home. I begged her to stay at Mt. Etna where we could at least hope the epidemic would pass us by, but, true to her headstrong nature, Bert volunteered with the Red Cross in Altoona and motored up there every day to do what she could to fight the enemy that had taken Andrew. I insisted that she keep to the tenant house and not interact with any of us in the hope of keeping the flu from invading Mt. Etna.

The end of the war brought the flu home in full force, when the returning soldiers, greeted with such joy and excitement, spread the flu far and wide. Health departments passed out gauze masks and entreated people not to gather in groups. Train passengers had to show a health certificate before boarding, and because of the war, doctors were in short supply. Will and Auntie Beth were called out of retirement to treat the sick as the death toll rose through the fall and winter.

I shook with fear for all I loved, confining Olivia to the manor house, haunted by the stories I'd heard of the smallpox epidemic that took the lives of my father's first family after the War Between the States. All of that had seemed vague and sad to me, but it was nothing compared to this terror that shook me to my roots. I was frantic in my resolve to protect Olivia, come what may.

The epidemic lasted through the fall and winter, affecting almost every household. People would fall ill one day and die the next. The suffering was unbelievable, hitting the young folks hardest, probably because they thought themselves to be immortal—having survived the war—and, anxious to resume their interrupted lives, they picked up their associations where they'd left off, courting, partying, dancing, doing all the things they were warned against. But youth is convinced of its indestructibility, so they danced.

Bert took the flu herself, but true to her nature, fought it off and went on caring for the sick. Auntie Beth wasn't so lucky. A frail eighty-four, she should have been prevented from any involvement with the sick, but no.

"I've lived a long and fruitful life. If I can do anything to help, I must. Better me than someone who hasn't lived." And so she passed away at the bedside of a sick returned soldier in December.

Will took sick as well, but younger than she by twelve years, he had more stamina and worked through his illness. Bert moved into their clinic and worked side by side with him through the spring of 1919. Once the epidemic dissipated, she stayed on, helping as needed, seemingly oblivious to anything but learning how to care for the sick. I didn't mind, for at least I didn't have to listen to her endless tirades about suffrage or worry over her influence on Olivia.

In the spring the epidemic began to wane—perhaps because practically everyone had contracted the flu and developed immunity. So busy with caring for the family and the village folk, I let my correspondence with Alex drift until one day in April I received a letter from Philadelphia in unfamiliar handwriting.

Dear Miss MacPhail,

My friend Alessandro Bodnar, pianist extraordinaire, has been taken from us by the influenza. He was a great friend to me, encouraging me in my musical career, and he often spoke of you with sparkling eyes and ready joy. When he was taken ill, he asked me to write to you and tell you that his love would not die with him, that he had written a composition for the piano and dedicated it to you. It is entitled, simply, "Sarah." I will play it at my debut piano concert in May, with a remembrance of Alessandro's incredible talent, memorialized in his love for you.

With great sadness and deep regret, I sign myself,

Raphael Giosa

So it was. Love came in at the door, and I could not keep hold of it. Elusive, fragile love.

Chapter 24

Olivia, 1925

Don't think I'm not grateful to Mama Sarah for taking me in when my mother drowned in the river. I was three then, and I can hardly remember any of it. And she's been a good mother to me, but I get it when Ned says she's bossy. It seems she doesn't like anything I like or want me to do anything I want to do. That's why I like Bert. She's up for anything—others' opinions be damned.

Whoops! Mama Sarah would be upset if she ever heard that word—or a host of others—escape my lips. I'm eighteen years old, ready to graduate and I have a lot of ideas about who and what I'm going to be, few, if any of which please Mama Sarah.

I thank Bert for that. She's the one who took me to all those suffrage meetings, and look at us now! Congress passed the Nineteenth Amendment in the spring of 1919. Then all it took was for the states to ratify it by the summer of 1920, and women got the vote. Bert was elated—celebrated with all her suffragette friends for a week. I wasn't old enough to vote in 1920, but I promise you I'll never miss another chance as long as I live

Mama Sarah flirted with the cause a little bit, but I think she was only trying to prove she was up with the times, and maybe trying to keep Bert from having all my attention. I did appreciate the effort she made, half-hearted though it was.

Bert's wholly dedicated to another cause now. Medicine. She went to the University of Pittsburgh to study after the flu epidemic. Now she's practicing medicine with Cousin Will in Altoona. He's almost eighty now, so I guess she'll have the practice to herself one of these days. Once Andrew was gone, she figured she could do as she pleased, but I sure do miss her. The last time I saw her, Sarah didn't want me to go over to the tenant house because she had a long list of chores for me to do that day. Seemed like she always had my schedule full when Bert was around. But Bert only came down to visit and rest a little a few times a year, so I went anyway, without telling Mama Sarah, 'cause I missed Bert so much.

It was just after the New Year, cold and blustery, so we sat on the settee by the fireplace in the tenant house, sipping tea and talking. Bert wanted to know what I was going to do after graduation.

"I don't know. Go to college, I guess. Mama Sarah has her heart set on that."

Bert grimaced. "It's not Mama Sarah's life. It's yours. Make your decision based on what *you* want, not what she wants."

"Well, I'm not sure what I want. I could go into medicine like you, but that doesn't really appeal to me. I could be a nurse or a secretary or a teacher. That's about all girls are supposedly suited for."

"Nonsense, Ollie. You can be anything you want. Don't hold yourself back, and don't let anyone else do it either."

I leaned forward, enfolding my tea cup in my hands to warm them. "Know what I'd really like to do? I'd like to be a reporter for a newspaper."

Bert pulled back, chin in, studying me with a faint smile. "Really? Where?"

"Anywhere. In a big city, maybe. I think it'd be fun to report on what's happening—be the first to know all about it."

"Oh, my God, Ollie, don't ever breathe a word of this to Sarah. She'd chain you to your bed."

I giggled. "I know. She'd never allow it, but . . .. Do you still have friends in New York?"

She leaned against the back of the settee, thoughtful. "Yes, I do. No one in the newspaper business, but you never know who knows who. I'll ask around."

It was the beginning of my quest for independence and adventure, the two things I thought I wanted most. I nurtured the dream, encouraged by Bert, hoping to tap her influence.

I kept my plans from Mama Sarah to spare her months of anguish. At that age I didn't want to even consider compromise, so I thought I'd just board a train for New York after graduation and let her know in a letter. That sounded slick and easy at the time, but things never work out the way you think they will.

Bert and I had our heads together planning my escape when Mama Sarah surmised there was a conspiracy afoot and came down on me one evening a few months before graduation. "Olivia, have you sent in your paperwork to Juniata?"

"Not yet. I'm not sure if I want to go there or not."

"Really? We've had this conversation before, and I thought we'd settled it."

"I don't know. I just can't get excited about it. I'd like to look around some more."

Mama Sarah folded the paper she was reading and laid it down on the settee beside her. "Well. I suppose you should take your time and be sure, but I certainly would prefer that you went to Juniata. It's close to home, and I went there, you know. Didn't graduate, but I still have a special place in my heart for the school."

"Why didn't you graduate?"

She hesitated, a sure sign she was thinking up a misleading substitute for the truth.

"Why . . . my mother died and I had to come home to take care of Ned."

I'll bet he loved that, I thought.

"Didn't you tell me once that you and my mother were roommates?'

"Yes. Yes, we were." Mama Sarah picked up the newspaper again and opened it, as though to dismiss, this line of questioning.

"Was she pretty? Do I look like her?"

She stopped reading and looked at me over her paper. "Yes, you do, dear. She was beautiful—dark haired with blue eyes, tall. All the young men were in love with her. I think I must have a picture of her somewhere. I'll see if I can find one."

I smiled at the thought of my mother, a beauty, popular with all the boys. I was no such thing. In fact most boys wanted little to do with me. Bert said it was because I was too smart for them. Made them uncomfortable. I didn't know, but it was a sore spot, nonetheless.

I'd never been told anything about my mother except that she drowned in the river with my baby brother when the foot bridge at Blair Four gave way. Curious now, I asked more questions, until Mama Sarah, looking frustrated cut me off.

"Really, dear, I think you should make up your mind to attend Juniata and be done with it." With that, she rose and went into the kitchen, leaving me to wonder about things she would obviously prefer I left alone.

I decided to ask Bert next time she came to visit. She'd gone to Juniata, too. She could tell me what I wanted to know. But she wouldn't be down for a visit until May, so I waited.

Bert's arrival was, as usual, full of fuss and flurry. She reclaimed the tenant house, opened all the windows and doors and went about sweeping and dusting, beating rugs and wiping windows. Glad for something to do, and for a chance to spend an afternoon with her, I helped with the cleaning.

As we swept, wiped and dusted, Bert stopped and leaned on her broom. "I hear you're going to my alma mater," she said.

"Maybe. I'm still not sure yet. Might just hop a train and go to New York—skip college."

"Your choice."

"Weren't you at Juniata when Mama Sarah went there?"

"Uh huh. Same class."

"Why'd she quit? She says it was because her mother died and she had to take care of Ned, but that doesn't seem to say it all. I think she's holding back, just using Ned for an excuse."

Bert leaned her broom against the wall and motioned for me to follow her outside where she sat down on a bench under one of the huge Weeping Willows. She patted a place beside her.

"What's she told you? How did this come up, anyway?"

"I was asking about why she quit, and about my mother, and she got all flummoxed and quit talking."

"Ummm. Well, my dear, I probably shouldn't be telling you this, but . . ."

The whole story came out, how Sarah and my mother were roommates and how Sarah was in love with this professor, and he dumped her and she came running home, humiliated. Then my mother married the professor and they ended up working the store at Blair Four. It did shed some light on why Mama Sarah didn't want to talk about it. So that's how it was. Knowing this made me hungry for one more bit of enlightenment. My father. The professor. Phillip Chamberlain.

"What about him?" I asked.

Bert frowned. "I don't think anyone knows where he is now. He's never come around. Sarah said once he was a professor at some college down east, but I don't know which." She reached out and took my hand. "I'm sorry, Ollie. He must have been a blackguard to leave you and never come back. I didn't know him well, but he had a reputation for loving and leaving. You've got to be glad Sarah took you in. She's been a good mother in spite of her foibles."

"I knew that's true, but I don't like the idea of having been a poor motherless waif, left to the charity of others, abandoned by my father."

"I know. It certainly doesn't square with my idea of who and what you are, but I don't think you'd find any satisfaction if you knew him. Some stones are better left unturned."

I knew she was right. I didn't really want to know him. More like punish him, but that still wouldn't take away the hurt.

I put Mama Sarah off until June when she insisted I send in my papers to Juniata, harping that it was probably already too late. I was feeling low—had been ever since I learned that piece of my history about this Phillip Chamberlain who'd sired me.

Ned and I talked about it some. We liked to get away and air our grievances once in a while. On this day we'd started out to go fishing, but we hadn't made it any farther than two Adirondack chairs on the front lawn. His take on my father was that he wasn't evil, just weak. Couldn't get along without someone falling all over him in blind admiration.

"I guess that's what happened to Sarah, though she never said anything about him to me. I just knew she'd been hurt and disappointed."

"Is that what made her think she had to run *your* life?"

"I guess so. She needed a distraction and I was it."

"You know, Ned, sometimes I wonder how you've put up with it all these years."

"It's not so bad now. She let loose of me when you came on the scene. Before that she was on me all the time. I wanted to run away from the time I was fifteen."

"Why didn't you?"

"Oh, my condition."

"Condition? What condition?"

He looked uncomfortable, and I didn't want to press him, so I just sat there looking at the grass until he spoke again.

"I don't know what you call it. I was painfully shy and withdrawn as a boy. I didn't know how to act around strangers, so I avoided them. Everyone thought I was slow, so they babied me, protected me. Papa and Mama were all right, but after they died, Sarah took over and treated me like a sick puppy."

"Sick puppy?"

"Some poor soul she had to watch over and take care of."

"I'll bet you hated that."

"Sure. I wanted to grow up and be a man, and Sarah stood in the way."

He stood up, brushed off his pants and took up his fishing rod. "This was my salvation, fishing. I could get away and be by myself and think. When Sarah was around, she battered my eardrums and beat down my self-confidence."

"Wow." I exhaled slowly. "No wonder you don't like her."

"I like her well enough. She thought it was the right thing to do—take care of me. She was just sure I couldn't get along without her to guide me. That was nonsense, but there was no convincing Sarah."

He motioned for me to follow, and we walked down along the river bank, stepping over roots and rocks, until we came to a lovely shaded hole where Ned flipped his line.

"I kept wishing she'd get married. Tried to get Richard to marry her lots of times. He always was sweet on her. But he was afraid of her too. Sarah was like that. You knew if you opposed her, it would be a hard fought battle, and I guess Richard didn't feel like fighting it. Anyway, you saved me. Once Sarah had you to dote on, she let up on me."

"Glad to be of assistance," I laughed.

"Yeah, but what's going to happen when you go away? She'll be back on me like a duck on a June Bug.

Chapter 25

Ned, 1925

Sarah complained she was worn out with raising Ollie and standing against Bert's constant opposition to everything she thought a young girl should be. I guess she was, but Ollie was growing up fast and would be gone before she knew it, and then she'd be sad to have no one to take care of. Ollie was eighteen and already graduated from high school in Williamsburg. Now college. She'd be finished there in four years, and then it would be marriage and moving away. I doubted we'd see much of her once she started college. She wouldn't want to come back to Mt. Etna when there was a whole world out there waiting for her to explore. Ollie was a smart girl, and full of pee and vinegar.

It sure would be lonely around here with her gone because Bert's visits were few and far between after she joined Will's practice in Altoona. That left Mt. Etna to Sarah and me and Richard. With no one else to boss, Sarah was soon back at me. Made me think sometimes I should just run away like I'd always talked about.

That's when I started to think maybe I should have a refuge—some place of my own where I could go when Sarah got too high-handed. The old stone carriage house still stood out back of the manor house, and I conjured a living quarters there, where I would be my own master. Not too far away, just far enough that I could live with my sovereignty in tact.

So I started to build it, a little at a time so as not to alarm Sarah. I partitioned off the old tack room, brought in a pot bellied stove, a cot and a chair. That was all there was at first, but as time went on, I enjoyed my freedom so much, I kept on making improvements until I had myself a cozy nest. Sarah didn't know what I was up to until I had it fixed right nice.

"What's this?" she asked when she happened out to the carriage house looking for a garden rake one morning.

"What's what?"

"Why this—this room. Is this your doing, Ned?"

I stood by the door and let her inspect it, proud of my accomplishment. "Yes, ma'am. It's my hidey place."

"Hidey place? Whatever do you need a hidey place for?"

"To get away from you."

"Get away from me? Stuff and nonsense. You've no need to get away from me." She moved to pull the door shut, but I put my foot in front of it.

"No, you don't. This is my place. And yes I do need to get away from you. You're a tyrant. You run everything. I want some time to myself."

Sarah turned in a huff and strode out the carriage house door. "We'll just see about this!"

I stood back in the doorway to my hidey place and smiled, arms crossed in defiance. Good for you, Sarie. You have it coming.

I still went over to Blair Four to see Marta sometimes but once Jacob got too big to tag after his mother, my meetings with him were mostly by chance. He fished in the river—it wasn't what it used to be—only catfish, suckers or carp. I wanted to teach him to fish for game fish—wanted him to know the thrill of catching a wily trout. But he didn't know me for anything but a sometime friend, and even though I asked him about his fishing exploits, and he was proud to tell me, it was no more than casual conversation.

He turned out to be a fine looking boy. Went to school at Blair Four, and finished at the top of his class. Once he'd gone through the eighth grade, I wanted to see him go to high school in Williamsburg, but I didn't think Andros would take kindly to sending him there, since his own children wouldn't have the means to go. Jacob ran with the Blair Four kids—a rough and unruly crowd—and I worried that those attachments would keep him in the quarry.

He'd wandered over to Mt. Etna on occasion, but the young folks around here and the ones from Blair Four didn't mix well so he didn't come around much. And the folks from the Sycamore Cottages had some burglaries, so, of course the blame was placed on the kids from Blair Four, deserved or not. I wished Jacob could know who he was and come and go as he pleased around here, but Sarah didn't even know him, and if she had, she'd have done her best to keep him a secret.

Jacob knew me as a friend to his family, but that friendship didn't extend to the rest of my people, so he never visited me when he came to Mt. Etna. I longed to tell him who I was and all about my family, but Marta was always afraid that might lead to trouble, so I kept my peace.

He did get to go to high school in Williamsburg. There was no school bus then, so he would have to board in town. I paid his board and asked that the school keep that a secret—send Marta a letter telling her that Jacob had won a scholarship and that his board was paid for the full year. She was so proud of him. I did the same thing every year he was in high school.

After that I planned to make sure he could go to college—didn't want him to end up working in a quarry all his life—so when the time came for college, I took my fly tying money down to Founder's Hall at Juniata College and paid the fees for my son. Again Marta got a letter of congratulations and was none the wiser.

I wondered how he'd feel if he knew who I was. Wondered what Marta had told him about his father. I guessed any child would be curious, but there was always the underlying dread that if he knew, he'd hate me for not marrying his mother and taking care of them. So I stayed in the background and hoped that someday . . . someday . . .

I liked to fish for Rainbows over in Fox Run because it was close to Blair Four and sometimes I'd walk through there on my way home in hopes of seeing Marta or Jacob. He was tall—taller than I was—and slight. His dark hair and striking blue eyes reminded me of a picture I'd seen of my Uncle John as a young man. The thing I liked best about him was that he was so friendly and direct. He'd walk right up to anyone and smile, offer his hand and start a conversation—look them in the eye, confident, assured. I was better than I used to be about meeting new people, but I'd never be as able as my son.

I stood under the bridge over Fox Run, a little upstream of the railroad underpass on a hot July day. The shade of the bridge and the cool water made it a perfect refuge for man and fish. I'd just caught a big Rainbow and stooped to release it, holding it gently in my hands for a while, stroking its colorful side. I always felt like I knew the fish, understood it, and it understood me. I might not have a great relationship with many people, but I got along just fine with fish.

"Are you going to let it go?"

The voice echoing under the bridge startled me. I looked up, peering toward the opening. There stood Jacob, silhouetted against the rectangle of light from outside.

"Yes, I always do. Don't you?"

He stepped in out of the sunlight, rod in hand, and stooped down beside me to get a better look at the trout. It flipped out of my hands and swam away under a concrete ledge, free once more.

"Oh, sorry."

I smiled. "No need. I've caught my share." Then, happy to spend even a moment with him, I rose, took out a felt of flies I'd tied and held them out to him.

"Want to try one of these?"

He grinned and took a felt of flies out of his own pocket. "I think I've got one of those."

"Where'd you get them?" I asked.

"My mom gets them for me when she goes to town. She says you know more about fishing than anyone around here."

Marta. My beautiful, wonderful Marta, still taking care of me. I turned away, dug a clean white cotton handkerchief out of my pocket and wiped my brow. "So you like to fish, do you?"

"Yep."

"Come on, I'll show you one of the best holes in the county."

"Trout?"

"Rainbows and Brownies. Some of the biggest."

I led the way along the bank, upstream almost a quarter of a mile. The boy followed, patient, respectful. We arrived at a bend in the creek where a huge Weeping Willow spread its boughs, shading a flat rock cantilevered over the water. I stepped back and gave him space.

"Right there at the tip of the rock. Put her in above and let her drift past."

"Which fly?"

"You pick. I think you know your flies."

He stepped back and thoughtfully considered before selecting one and tying it on. Standing away from the shore, he flicked his line out just where I'd directed and let it drift downstream. Suddenly a dark shape darted out from under the rock and nabbed the fly, quick, decisive, determined. Jacob jerked the line to set the hook and proceeded to play the fish, gently, but firmly. A big Brownie, it put up a fight, but the hook was set and I watched with satisfaction as the boy showed patience, moving the fish ever closer to the shore.

I stood by with my landing net, wanting to give him all the time and space he needed, but apprehensive that he'd manage to bring it in. Just within a foot of the shore, the trout stopped struggling, lay on its side and breathed while Jacob and I watched it. He turned to me.

"It's the biggest one I ever caught—saw, for that matter."

In the excitement of the moment, he reached for the net, turned his ankle on a rock and fell down on one knee, dropping his rod. Without thinking, I scooped it up and brought the fish to the net. I landed it and stood there holding it up for him to see. Then, realizing I'd stolen his joy, I apologized.

"Sorry, son. I didn't mean to get in your way." I handed the net to him and watched him lower it into the water, lift the fish out and let it slip through his hands back under its rock.

"I'm really sorry. Should have stood by and watched. I don't know what I was thinking."

"It's okay, Mr. Ned. You wanted to help. That's what dads are for."

Caught unawares, it felt like he'd punched me in the gut. I looked at him in disbelief, my head awhirl. "You know?"

"Yes, sir. I know."

"But, how?"

"My mother told me. She thought I needed to know. I was always asking her about my father, and she told me a lot, so that I got suspicious when you'd come to visit. When I asked her point blank if you were my father, she said yes."

"When, Jacob?"

"When I was about twelve. She waited until I was old enough to understand a little. She told me all about how you used to sit up in a tree and watch her—and about the cabin in the woods and her brothers beating you up. She even took me over and showed me what's left of the cabin."

"Does your uncle know?"

"No. My mother goes out of her way not to irritate him. He's been good to us."

Standing on the creek bank looking at my son, I struggled to put it all together. Marta. My dear, loving Marta. She'd told him so he'd know who he was and let him decide for himself what to do about it. I turned back to face him.

"What now?"

"I guess we just go on as we always have. You stop by for a visit now and then. We meet by chance here and there. When I'm a man, I'll be free to befriend whoever I want."

"Jacob."

"Yes, sir?"

"Are you angry with me? Do you think I've cheated you?"

"No. I've a good mother and a good life. I think I understand how it was with you. My mother still loves you."

Overcome with relief, I sat down on the big flat rock, hugged my knees and let the tears roll down my face onto my trousers. My son. My son. It was like he'd been gone and now he was home.

"Sir?"

"Don't call me sir. I'm your father."

"Yes, sir. I mean, I can't just call you Papa yet. It'll take some time to get comfortable. But don't be sad. It all turns out right in the end."

I rose, wiping my eyes with my handkerchief, and reached for him. He came into my arms, shy but willing. I held him for the first time, kissed his cheek and cried some more.

Chapter 26

Richard, 1928

I woke up early, before dawn, with the smell of smoke in the air. I went out to check the mill and outbuildings, but it was plain the smoke was coming from down river. The whole valley was clouded over, so I knew it must be a big fire. I started down the tracks toward Blair Four as the smell got stronger and the cloud of smoke over the village thickened. Somebody's house. People were milling around, coughing against the smoke, dragging things out of the smoldering ruin. Whose house?

"Andros Rodich."

"Anyone hurt?"

No answer. Just a jerk of the head toward a stack of charred bodies, covered with sheets.

"Oh, my God. How many?"

"Eight so far, but there's more. It's too hot to get them out yet."

"Oh, my God."

An official-looking man wearing hip boots waded among the ashes, notebook in hand. I recognized him as Dr. Simpson from Williamsburg, counting the dead.

"Anything I can do, Doc?" I asked.

He paused, chewed his pencil and gave me a hopeless look. "If you can get to a phone, you can call in town to the undertaker. Have him locate some more coffins and send them out. I count ten now, maybe more."

"Sure. Be glad to."

I knew Andros Rodich was Marta's brother, knew Marta lived with him. I wasn't sure whether Jacob would have been there or not, but hoped he wasn't. He was close to finishing at Juniata College. This would be devastating for him.

Andros always was a little on the tough side. Had to have things his own way. He was good to Marta and Jacob, but he expected obedience. Same with his wife and children—nine of them—all dead now. And all because of that Jan Yanish. Stupid, worthless son-of-a-bitch. Couldn't take no for an answer.

Cassandra—Cassie—Andros's oldest daughter, a dark haired beauty by any measure, followed around by half the boys in Blair Four in hope of a smile or a kind word, had finally made up her mind to marry Klaus Faber, a German newcomer. That's what made Jan Yanish snap. He was courting Cassie until Klaus came along, and he took rejection hard. The wedding was yesterday, and true to form everyone in Blair Four above the age of twelve got drunk. I know. Prohibition. But it'd never stopped them yet.

The whole family, all of them including Klaus, sleeping in Andros's house—upstairs, downstairs, wherever. Marta wouldn't have been drunk, nor, I doubt, Jacob, if he was there. But they'd all stayed up late and were in a stupor of sleep when someone— no one saw, but we all know it was Yanish—set the house on fire. Since everyone in town was in the same condition, no one noticed the fire until the whole house was engulfed and there was nothing to do but watch it burn. They didn't have much of a fire company—just one engine, and, honestly, I don't think anyone was sober enough to operate it. The wooden structure went up like tinder.

It took almost a week to identify all the bodies. There were thirteen. Thirteen people burned to death in a senseless act of revenge. Jan Yanish was arrested and jailed, awaiting the outcome of the investigation. Some said the fire could have started in the stove, by accident, but nobody believed that.

Ned was beside himself, in a frenzy to find out if Jacob had been there, already sure that Marta was. He went about half-mad, until a car drove up from Huntingdon and Jacob, emerged, rushed to his father's arms, grieving for his mother. When Doc Simpson put up the list of the dead, identified by various means, Marta Rodich was one of them. Ned went a little crazy.

He'd grown up a lot since his courting days—turned into a pretty stable, sensible man, with only a slight tendency toward eccentricity. People barely thought him odd anymore, but not even the most hard-hearted, rational, emotionless among us could withhold pity for him and Jacob. Marta had always been kind and simple and loving a good and devoted mother.

After Ned read the list of the dead, he turned and walked out of the village, head down, trudging along resolute. I looked to see if Jacob would go after him, but the boy stood motionless, head down, grieving. I called to Ned, but he didn't answer, just kept walking, so I followed him all the way to the manor house, where he mounted the steps, grim faced.

Sarah was standing in the kitchen helping Mrs. Beck knead the bread. Mrs. Beck was getting on in years, so Sarah helped her sometimes. Ned walked up to her, raised a fist and smashed it into the dough.

"You! You did this! You thought you could run my life, keep me on your well-defined straight and narrow path. Dictate my every move. Well, you've done it and what has it gotten you? Marta is dead. If she'd been here, living with me as my wife, she'd still be alive. See what you've done?"

He pounded the dough with both fists, beating it down, his face red with rage.

"No, Ned. No. I didn't . . ."

"Yes, you did, Sarah. You thought you knew best. Hounded me, bossed me, never gave me a minute's peace, and now the only woman I've ever loved is dead."

"But, Ned, you needed guidance."

"No. You needed guidance. You thought you knew it all, but you didn't. You didn't know anything. If I'd gone my own way, we'd have been all right. Marta and me. and Jacob."

Sarah looked past him at me, pleading. "Please don't blame me. I only did what I thought was right."

I chose to stay out of it. There was a lot that needed to be said—that Sarah needed to hear, and I hoped Ned would say it all.

He kept punching the bread dough his fists sticking to it, dragging it up in globs. Tears steamed down his face, sobs racking his body. Now he picked up the basin of dough and hurled it across the room. It landed against the wall, shattering plaster, spreading the dough over the floor. Mrs. Beck drew in her breath, a hand to her face.

Sarah scurried over and bent down to pick up the basin, scooping up the dough as though it could be saved. Tears ran down as she raised her face to her brother.

"I didn't mean it, Ned. I thought I was helping you."

"Well, don't help me anymore. Please."

He stood watching her gather up the dough, kneeling on the floor, tears coursing down both of their faces. She looked up at him. "Forgive me, Ned? Can you ever, please?"

He lurched past the table and knelt beside her on the floor, reached for her and gathered her into his arms. Together, they cried, holding onto each other, their heads pressed together. I stepped into the dining room to let them work their way through it. Mrs. Beck followed me, her hands shaking under her apron.

"Sit down, Mrs. Beck. Let them go. They'll work it out."

"If only Miss Sarah had better sense. She didn't mean to," she said.

***

Ned's way of recovering from the loss was to get away by himself, work like a dog, and grieve his heart out. Jacob returned to Huntingdon to finish his last term at Juniata.

I kept a pretty close eye on Ned in those terrible days after the fire—at Sarah's request—just to make sure he was all right. He was. Actually, over time he got along better than he ever had, knowing his son had been spared. He avoided Sarah—didn't talk to her any more than necessary, kept to himself, and helped me clear brush, mend fences, repair roofs, whatever was needed. He took his meals in the manor house, with Sarah, but retreated to his hidey place overnight. It seemed to work for him.

One day, as we worked on the fences, I told Ned what had happened to Jan Yanish. "You remember my cousin, Daniel Trethaway, from Huntingdon?"

"I guess so. Maybe."

"Well, he and I visit some, and the other day we got to talking about the fire. You know, people still talk about it—how Jan Yanish got away with it after the grand jury couldn't find enough evidence to charge him."

"Yeah?"

"Well, he left the area as soon as they let him out of jail. Went to Chicago to work in the meat packing plants."

Ned stood up to ease the pain in his back from bending over. "Uh huh."

"Daniel says there was an article in the local paper, off the wire service from Chicago. It said a fellow by the name of Jan Yanish was working on the killing floor, you know, where they knock the cows on the head with a sledge hammer. Well, one of the cows wasn't killed, only stunned, and it took off running all over the killing floor, slipping and sliding in blood, and it slammed into Yanish, gored him right through the gut and killed him."

"Fit destiny for a demon of hell."

Chapter 27

Ollie, 1928

I knew Jacob Rodich in high school and at Juniata, but I didn't know he was Mr. Ned's son. That was a whole revelation that came out in one of my happy tête-à-têtes with Bert under the Weeping Willow tree. She still came down to Mt. Etna on occasion, and if I knew she was coming, I'd be sure and get home for the weekend.

"I met this boy," I began, giving Bert a look that said it all.

"Oh, no! Don't tell me! Ollie's in love!"

I smiled, a little embarrassed, because Bert, always the modern woman, saw love as a passing fancy that only the empty headed would take as permanent.

"Yes. Maybe. I mean, for now, anyway."

"Well, tell me about him. Tell it all, now, Ollie, don't spare any details."

"His name is Jacob. Jacob Rodich."

She stood up, hands to her face, clapped her cheeks in amazement. "Jacob Rodich? Jacob Rodich? Where is he from? Blair Four?"

I nodded, perplexed by her reaction. "Yes. Blair Four. Why?"

"Oh, my dear. What a strange turn of events. He goes to Juniata, does he?"

"Yes, we've been in classes together for years. I've always sort of liked him, but now . . ."

"Did you know his mother died in that terrible fire at Blair Four last April?"

"Not when it happened, but afterward. What has you so wrought up?"

She took my hand and led me to her favorite bench. "Sit, dear. Has he told you anything about his father?"

"No. Just that he was raised by his mother, and he's only recently gotten to know his father."

"Ollie. His father is Ned. Ned MacPhail."

Struck dumb by the revelation, I shook my head in disbelief. "Jacob? Ned's son? How did that happen?"

"In the usual way, my dear, but it's a poignant story. I'll leave it to Ned to tell you, but how long have you and Jacob been . . . ?"

"Not very long. Just this term, really. We'd started to see each other around the end of last term. It was starting to get serious in the early spring, then the fire. Jacob turned to me for comfort. I helped him grieve, listened to his story, held him up when it got too much. He's a wonderful man, Bert."

She hugged me close. "Oh, Ollie, what a story! What a story. You'll have to bring him around. When can I meet him?"

"How about tomorrow? He's coming to see me tomorrow."

Jacob's arrival at Mt. Etna the next day heralded a new chapter in so many lives. For him and me, it was the announcement of our betrothal; for Bert it was a celebration of joy for those she loved; for Ned it was the discovery that his son and I were to be married, and for Mama Sarah, it was another difficult adjustment. She couldn't run my life anymore, either.

Once all the introductions were made and the relationships straightened out, Jacob rose and announced our engagement to the whole company. I noticed Richard Trethaway standing in the background looking happy and just a little thoughtful. Hmmm.

Chapter 28

Richard, 1928

Forty-seven years old, and what did I have to show for my life? A worn out flour mill that few farmers ever used anymore, a poor cottage that belonged to somebody else, and no joy. I should have married a long time ago. God knew that. I'd waited around all these years for Sarah MacPhail, the most hard-headed woman on earth, and that was the God's honest truth. I wondered what she'd say if I just up and got married. I could have, you know. Louisa Berendt would have had me, no doubt. Living alone with two brothers, cooking and cleaning for them, she'd probably have been glad of a chance to get away. Young enough to give me a son, yet, she was, too.

But I guessed you couldn't just decide to marry somebody for convenience or to satisfy some dream. I couldn't, at least. I'd loved Sarah since were kids, and I knew, in some way, she loved me. Still, after all that had happened, I felt a deep need to fill the emptiness while I still could, so I took myself up to the manor house one Sunday afternoon in August, scrubbed, brushed and polished and buoyed up with a shot or two of Irish whiskey I'd bought at Water Street years ago, for just such a purpose.

Sarah greeted me at the front door with a perplexed look. "Richard! I thought it was some stranger. Why are you coming in this way?"

"I come on personal business."

"Oh? What sort of personal business? Come in, anyway. I hope you're not going to tell me you're moving away or something."

She led the way into the parlor, a room I'd rarely been privileged to visit except to carry in fire wood. I stood with my hat in my hands, looking around at the pictures of dead MacPhails hanging on all four walls. Just looking at them made me wonder what I'd been thinking, coming here on this errand.

"Sit down, Richard. Can I ask Mrs. Beck to bring you some tea?"

"Yes, ma'am. Thank you."

"Ma'am? Oh, dear. This does sound serious."

She rang a little bell by her chair and Mrs. Beck appeared from the kitchen with a quizzical look at me.

"Tea, please, Mrs. Beck. And if you've any of those sugar cookies Richard likes, some of them, too."

She sat prim in her chair looking at me while I cast about for a way to begin.

"Richard, have you been drinking?"

"No ma'am. I don't drink. You know that."

"Hmmm. I could swear I smelled liquor when you walked in the door."

"No, ma'am." I felt pretty foolish for having needed fortification for my errand.

We sat quiet, looking at each other until Mrs. Beck returned with the tea tray and a plate of cookies.

"Well, are you going to tell me what brings you here today, or do you want me to guess?"

"No, ma'am. I . . . I . . . Well, you see, we're not getting any younger, you and I, and I was thinking . . . I mean, people need other people. In their lives, I mean. Other people to help them and support them and be there when they need them . . ."

"Ye-es? I know that. And I've always appreciated that you stayed here at Mt. Etna and helped me through all the hard times. You've been a rare friend, Richard."

"Yes, ma'am. That's what I wanted to talk about. Friendship."

She poured the tea and passed me the plate of cookies. "Friendship? Why of course. We've always been friends, you and I. I doubt I've ever had a better friend or a more faithful one."

Emboldened by that response, I plunged forward, full speed. "Yes, that's right, Sarah, so I came here to tell you that I'm getting married."

"Married? To whom?"

"To you, Sarah MacPhail, if you'll have me."

There. I'd done it. A huge relief passed over me. The asking was the hard part, but at least I'd done it. Now all I had to do was wait, and even if she said no, I'd done it. Then too, Louisa Berendt still loomed as a possibility, just in case.

Sarah frowned like she wondered what had come over me. "Married? Why, Richard, I never saw you in that light. You're more like my brother—the best one, I might add—but I never . . ."

"Well, you should consider it. I could be more help around here if I had a stake in the place. You still own my lease hold, but there really isn't much milling business these days. Anyway, Sarah, I think you could use full time help, you know."

With that I rose and put on my hat. "Think about it, Sarah. If you won't have me, there are others who would, so just let me know." I strode from the room and out the front door before my legs could turn to jelly.

Sarah

Well, would you have believed that Richard Trethaway would ask me to marry him? I was flabbergasted, to say the least. I like Richard—always have—but marry him? It'd been ten years since Alex died, and I still thought about him. What might have been. Still, I had my memories and my daughter. I called her mine, for, even though she came from a different mother, she was as close as if I'd borne her. My only intent was to see her launched into a good life, and now it seemed that was assured. Olivia would become Jacob's wife in September. Ned seemed content enough, doing what he'd always done, and Bert was happily established as Will's partner in Altoona, still delighted that women finally got the vote.

So Olivia was my main focus and she'd gone and found herself a husband right close to home. Jacob planned to open a law practice in Huntingdon and Olivia, of all things, had talked Bert into buying the Huntingdon Sentinel, the daily newspaper and letting her run it! I wondered how she'd manage when the little ones came, then reminded myself that it wasn't my affair.

Ned always thought he had me fooled. Thought I didn't know who Jacob was, but I knew. I'd always known. Knew Ned sneaked off over there to watch over him as he grew up. I never said anything because Ned felt bad enough about the whole business, but he'd come a long way, since those days—mostly grown out of those traits that made him so odd as a youngster. He actually made a pretty good living tying flies. Had a reputation for the best lures around, and orders came from all over the country. That's why I wasn't surprised when Ned went off to Huntingdon with his money in a cigar box and paid the fees to send Jacob to college.

What did surprise me was Richard Trethaway asking me to marry him. I guess he just got tired of waiting around for me to notice him. I did notice him. Still do. Probably should have married him a long time ago. Saved us both a lot of grief. He never complained, though. Just plodded along doing what had to be done, taking care of me and Mt. Etna as if we were his own.

I was born into a family of property and I felt the yoke on my shoulders. Thought I had to take care of it myself. No one was going to do it for me. Certainly not my two brothers. Andrew went off to war, and Ned stayed at home and fished, so Sarah had it all. Sarah and Richard, bless him. I thought maybe I'd better head him off before he went and did something foolish, like marrying Louisa Berendt, who everyone knew was a shrew.

Richard gave me ample time to think about his marriage proposal. Except for daily chores, he didn't come around for almost a month. I was beginning to wonder if he was having second thoughts when he appeared at the front door again on another Sunday afternoon.

"Good day, Sarah. I wonder whether you've given any consideration to my proposal of marriage." He stood outside on the porch, looking brushed and polished again, holding a small nosegay of violets that he thrust at me as I opened the screen.

"Richard, come in. Yes, I've given it much consideration. Come in. Sit down."

He followed me into the parlor and waited while I found a small vase for the flowers and took them to the kitchen for water. When I returned he was standing looking out the window, hands behind his back.

"I know I don't have much to offer," he began. "And I'm not an educated man, but I know you and your family and Mt. Etna, so there's nobody better suited to help you get along."

I nodded. "You're right. You do know me better than anyone else. And I've always relied on you for so much. So I've talked this over with Ned and Olivia—the only ones left to talk about it anymore. Ned has always been your advocate, so there was no need to convince him, and Olivia is Ned's disciple. So, yes, Richard. I will marry you, if you still want me."

He turned and looked at me as though he wasn't sure he'd heard right. "You will? Really? Why, Sarah, I'm honored."

"Aren't you going to do anything but talk?" I asked. With that he stepped across the room in one stride and took me into his arms. It felt right to be there, and I wondered why I'd never been there before. I breathed in his scent, so familiar over the years, so pleasing. He held me for a long time—I didn't want to be the first to let go—his arms strong and sheltering. I'd wanted that for so long—maybe forever—without realizing it.

"Oh, Richard, thank you. Thank you for so much over the years, and for this gift."

"Now I'm sorry I waited so long."

"So am I, but let's not waste any more time. Let's drive up to Hollidaysburg and get married tomorrow."

The drive to Hollidaysburg took about a half hour, the application for a license about as much and the ceremony itself in the rectory of the Presbyterian Church only fifteen minutes. There it was. Done.

Folks marveled at how resolute we'd been once the decision was made. Put it off for decades and then in one day it became a fait accompli. Driving home late that afternoon, we chuckled at ourselves.

"Aren't we the adventurers?" I asked Richard.

He reached over and patted my hand. "Yes, we are. I'm proud of you—reminds me of something Bert would do!"

I looked askance at him and smiled. "Yes, it does. Next thing you know I'll be running for office!"

Chapter 29

Sarah, 1930

When that terrible fire happened over at Blair Four, I must say I was relieved in a way—not for the loss of Marta, no, never. But there was just a bit of relief that we didn't have any connection to that place anymore. That was all right with me.

Ned was devastated, of course. Anyone would be. He hid himself away in his own world, grieving, shutting out everyone but Jacob. I tried to reach out to him, but there was no talking to him. So I asked Richard to keep track of him, and he did the only thing he knew would help. He put Ned to work, and between the two of them they did everything needed to bring the manor house and its immediate environs back from the brink of dilapidation. The little house where my grandparents had started married life almost a hundred years ago stood empty now that Tess had passed away. So Richard and Ned moved right on to refurbishing it as well

Blair Four itself was destined for oblivion. The orders from Pittsburgh and Johnstown ran out the next year, and the owners decided to close it down. They moved all the people out and took their equipment away. All that was left was the skeletons of the workers' houses—bare and empty. I can't say I was sorry. For me Blair Four held a lot of sad memories—Phillip and Claire, Marta,

Ned getting beaten up, and the fire. I was just as glad to see it go, even though for some I guess it was home and hearth.

I'm grateful that Richard and I are approaching old age as a couple. Well, I guess maybe we've always been a couple in the sense of caring about each other. One word from me and Richard would have asked me to marry him years ago. Truth to tell, I wish I had. He's always been stalwart. My best friend and helper.

Richard, March, 1936

Looked like there was weather afoot. It'd been a harsh winter, but the past few days had been a break, except for rain, rain, rain. There was plenty of snow to melt, so we didn't really need all this rain at one time to mix with the melting snow. Looked like we were in for it, though. Ned was across the river, rebuilding the cabin where he and Marta had conceived Jacob. He'd been living in his hidey place ever since Jacob and Ollie got married and moved to Huntingdon. I guess he thought it was time he got himself a real home. It meant a lot to him, fixing up the cabin. I expected him to move over there sometime. So, as the rain continued, I began to think maybe I'd better get across the river while I still could and see if I could entice him into coming home. The water was rising about a foot an hour, and there was no end to the rain.

I poled the boat across and slogged my way up the old trail to the cabin. It looked pretty bedraggled with the rain beating down and the trees bare of leaves.

"Halloo, Ned!'

No answer.

"Halloo, Ned!" Louder.

The cabin door opened a crack, and Ned peeked out.

"Richard, come on in."

The roof wasn't tight yet, so I entered to find pails and pans set everywhere under the leaks. The ceiling bowed with the weight of the rain, and the fire smoldered as the rain fairly poured down the chimney.

"Think we'd better get you out of here."

"Why?"

"Radio forecasts more rain, and with the river already up over its banks my guess is your cabin might not make it."

"Really? You think it won't let up soon? I think it will."

"Makes no difference what you think. I barely got over here, and I'm damned if I'm going to wait around here jawing with you. Get your coat and let's go."

Ned stood in the middle of the room among his pails and pans, looking around at the four walls he'd worked so hard to restore. For him it was a shrine to Marta, the love of his life, and Jacob, his pride and joy. "This is where Marta and I used to meet. We made love here."

"Yes. I know, but she wouldn't want you to stay here and get washed away by the flood. Come on, Ned. We gotta go."

"Seems a shame to leave it." Ned pulled on his boots, lifted his shotgun from its pegs on the wall, picked up his mackinaw and straightened up, looking around. "All right. If I have to go, I guess I'll go. But I'll be back."

We slogged down the path to the boat and found it already riding about a foot higher than when I'd left it. My pole was barely long enough to reach the bottom, and the current almost ripped it out of my hands more than once. I leaned into it with all my might, Ned rising to give me a hand. Our progress was slow, and we lost ground to the current so that we landed about a quarter mile downstream and had to walk back in the rain. We left the boat. No place to tie it up that it wouldn't get washed away.

Ned and I stopped at the mill cottage to take one last look. The river was already lapping at the door, and the rain still fell in a steady downpour. I'd grown up there, slept there every night of my life until Sarah and I got married. I looked around, shook my head, and closed the door. Ned gave me a pat on the back, his way of telling me he understood.

The mill itself sat precariously at the mouth of Roaring Run, which was now living up to its name. The mill wheel hung lopsided, whipped by the current, and the raging river was already lashing at the underpinnings of the old five-story building.

Across the old canal, the railroad bed was under water, so there'd be no trains for a while. We slogged our way back to the manor house, where Sarah greeted Ned with a kiss on the cheek and I settled in front of the fireplace in the parlor to dry out.

The damage was catastrophic. All the empty houses over at Blair Four were swept away—nothing left but the foundations. Ned's cabin was gone, washed away, log by log, until only the chimney and one corner wall remained as it had been when he and Marta had their tryst. The bridges at Blair Four, Carlim, Cove Forge and Williamsburg were all washed out, and hundreds of people had lost their homes and everything they owned. Illness followed the flood, for wells were contaminated and there was no clean water.

We worked hard to clean up afterwards, to bring things back to the way they'd been. But for some, there was no coming back.

The Great Depression had already taken the fight out of them. People struggled to regain their equilibrium with little work and less money. I was everlasting tired of getting wet and drying out by the time the flood waters receded, and I couldn't seem to get over my weariness.

I took to my bed to rest and recover, and now I come to the end of my narrative. Life is still good. Nothing ever changes, but everything does.

Sarah

The 1936 flood took more than property. It took the life of the man I'd come to love beyond measure. Richard took pneumonia and died within a month of the flood. I mourned him for the rest of my life—my friend, my lover, my touchstone. After not quite eight short years of marriage, I was alone again. Well, not entirely alone. There we were, Ned and I, as we'd started out. Ned still fished and I kept house. Mrs. Beck had decided to go live in town with her daughter after the flood, and I knew I was too old to train a new cook, so we got along without. Our fortunes were barely good enough to keep us comfortable, and the specter of taxes haunted my dreams, but we settled in to make the best of what was left to us.

I'd heard my mother say once that a loss is worse than a lack. I think that's so for Ned and me. If we'd been born poor and humble, without property and a sense that we were somebody, life would have been different. Not having is one thing. Having and losing is another thing entirely, and that goes for people and property alike.

Chapter 30

Sarah, 1948

I spent my life in fear that I would be the last MacPhail and that its future or lack of it rested on me. Well, it has come to pass, but I've forced myself to believe that no fault lies with me. Rather, I have been a faithful steward, doing my best to keep and preserve. My dear brother Ned went away and left me as he always threatened to do, found on the bank of Roaring Run, fishing rod in hand and a monstrous Brown trout on his line. That was three years ago, and much has happened since then.

I came to the conclusion that I couldn't keep living in the manor house—too big, too old, too drafty. So I moved back into the little house where Grandma Ellie lived when I was a child and where that same Grandma Ellie and her husband, Adam MacPhail, started life in Mt. Etna a hundred and fifty years ago.

The little house is just the right size for me and filled with memories. Most everyone is gone now. I've sold the whole village—and the manor house because it is too much for me to take care of and the taxes keep coming. I hope there'll be something left for Olivia and Jacob when I die, but if there isn't, that is as it must be.

I've thought a lot about those who've gone before, and instead of lamenting the loss of it I've come to realize that we are all just tenants in our various worlds—allowed to hold onto things for whatever time is allotted to us. When we pass, ownership passes on, as well. But there are things that endure. Things like memories written down, the curiosity of future generations, respect for what once was. There will always be those who pass by and wonder what this place was—who built this beautiful house of Pennsylvania limestone? Who worked to produce iron in that old furnace? And I know there will always be someone who knows, because of people who work diligently to keep the past—store it in dusty ill-equipped, ill-funded local libraries where the curious can unearth it, repeat it, pass it on.

Jacob comes to visit me once a week, and we sit in my snug little downstairs room and talk. I do most of the talking, while he listens and asks me questions. He brings a big, awkward recording machine—says he's taping what I say. I hope it lasts and he can pass it on to his children—there are three of them now.

More than that, I hope he puts it into a book and keeps it so the world will not forget this place—will wonder and perhaps imagine what this ghost of a town, must have been like in its prime. People coming and going. Canal boats hauling iron to market, shirtless men working the furnace and forge, children going to school, women hanging out laundry.

I belonged here, and it was left to me to tell the story. I know Jacob will write it someday. All the stories of life and love and struggle and hardship. All the stories of the people who lived in and loved this place.

Mt. Etna. An uncommon, remarkable, wondrous and marvelous place where people lived and worked, made iron, built a nation, forged a future.

I do not grieve its loss, for it has made its mark and will live on in history as long as there are people who look back and wonder.

About the Author

Judith Redline Coopey's interest in history can be traced to her father, an avid reader and student of history. Born in Altoona, Pennsylvania, Ms. Coopey holds degrees from the Pennsylvania State University and Arizona State University. She began writing at the age of eleven, when it occurred to her that she would like to become "a lady that writes books." Throughout her life she has written—an essay here, a magazine article there, a short story someplace else, but with her retirement from teaching history in the Mesa Public Schools, she turned to writing as a serious pursuit.

The youngest of eight children, she was the first and only one to graduate from college. Her marriage led to many adventures, including two years residence in Germany, fifteen in Wisconsin, and more than thirty-three in Arizona, where she now resides.

Her accomplishments are many, including founding a library in a small Wisconsin town, honors at writing conferences, a teaching career that spanned more than twenty years, raising two children, and enjoying two grandchildren.

Her first book, *Redfield Farm,* is the story of the Underground Railroad in Bedford County, Pennsylvania, inspired by the possibility that her Quaker ancestors may have been involved in the efforts to move fugitive slaves to Canada.

Her second book, *Waterproof,* addresses how people readjust their lives after a major catastrophe like the 1889 Johnstown Flood which nearly destroyed a whole city and took more than 2000 lives.

Looking for Jane, her third historical novel, is a quest for love and family in the 1890s, brought to life through the eyes of Nell, a young girl convinced that Calamity Jane is her mother.

Her most recent work, *The Juniata Iron Trilogy,* is a three-volume family saga set against the background of the iron industry in the 19th century. Volume One, *The Furnace,* and Volume Two, *Brothers,* precede the current Volume Three, *Full Circle.* The trilogy tells the story of three generations of the MacPhail and Trethaway families through more than 150 years on an iron plantation at Mt. Etna, Pennsylvania.

Ms. Coopey has spent her life reading, researching and loving history. As a teacher, researcher and author, she finds her inspiration in the rich history of Pennsylvania and in bringing to light stories of the lives of those who have gone before.

Redfield Farm

For Ann and Jesse Redfield, Quaker brother and sister, their hatred of slavery is as hard as Pennsylvania limestone. Ann's devotion to her older brother runs deep, so when he gets involved in the Underground Railroad, Ann asks no questions. She joins him in the struggle. Together they lie, sneak, masquerade and defy their way past would-be enforcers of the hated Fugitive Slave Law.

Their dedication to the cause leads to complicated relationships with their fellow Quakers, pro-slavery neighbors, and with the fugitives themselves. When Jesse returns from a run with a deadly fever, accompanied by a fugitive, Josiah, who is also sick and close to death, Ann nurses both back to health. But precious time is lost, and Josiah, too weak for travel, stays the winter at Redfield Farm. Ann becomes his teacher, friend and confidant. When disappointment shakes her to her roots, she turns to Josiah for comfort, and comfort leads to intimacy. The result, both poignant and inspiring, is life-long devotion to each other and to their cause.

Redfield Farm is a tale of compassion, dedication and love, steeped in the details of another time but resonant with implications for today's world.

The author brings a deep understanding of the details of the Underground Railroad, which lends authenticity and truth to this tale of a live well-lived and a love well-founded.

Waterproof

Fifty years after an earthen dam broke and sent a thirty-foot wall of raging destruction down on the city of Johnstown, Pennsylvania, Pamela McRae looks back on the tragedy with new perspective. This fast-moving retrospective propels the reader forward much as did the flood itself.

When the Johnstown flood hit, it wiped out Pam's fondest hopes, taking her fiancé and her brother's lives and her mother's sanity, and within a year her father walked away, leaving his daughter—now the sole support of her mother—to cope with poverty and loneliness.

The arrival of Katya, a poor Hungarian girl running away from an arranged marriage, finally gives Pam the chance she needs to get back into the world; Katya can care for her mother, and Pam can go to work for the *Johnstown Clarion* as a society reporter.

Then Davy Hughes, Pam's fiancé before the flood, reappears and, instead of being the answer to her prayers, further complicates her life. Someone is seeking revenge on the owners of the South Fork Fishing and Hunting Club, the millionaires who owned the failed dam. And Pam is afraid Davy has something to do with it.

Looking for Jane

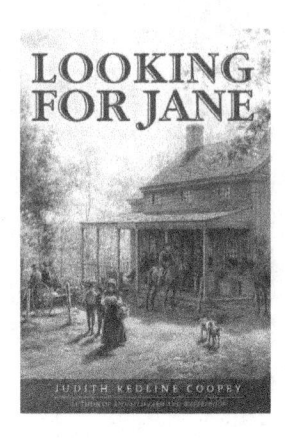

"The nuns use this as their measuring stick: who your people are. Well, what if you don't have no people? Or any you know of? What then? Are you doomed?" This is the nagging question of fifteen-year-old Nell's life. Born with a cleft palate and left a foundling on the doorstep of a Johnstown, Pennsylvania con-vent, she yearns for a place in the world—yearns to find her mother, whose name, she knows, was Jane.

When the Mother Superior tries to pawn her off to a mean looking farmer and his beaten down wife, Nell opts for the only alternative she can see: running away. She steals a rowboat, adopts a big, black dog and sets out downriver. A chance encounter with a dime novel heralding the exploits of Calamity Jane, heroine of the west, gives Nell the purpose of her life: to find Calamity Jane, her own true mother.

Thus begins Nell's quest, down rivers, up rivers and across the country all the way to Deadwood, South Dakota. Along the way she meets Jeremy Chatterfield, a handsome young Englishman who isn't particular about how he makes his way—as long as he doesn't have to work for it. Together they trek across the country, meeting characters as wonderful and bizarre as the adventure they seek, and learning about themselves and the world along the way.

This coming of age novel is a story of stubborn determination, self-discovery, adventure beyond measure, acceptance, and love—always love—the foundation of everything.

You'll take Nell with you to that special place where you keep the best characters. She'll stick with you, beat you down, buoy you up, and teach you a thing or two about life. You'll wonder at her single mindedness, her patience, and her courage—but you won't forget her. Not for a long time.

The Juniata Iron Trilogy
Book One – The Furnace

Elinor Bratton is young, beautiful, privileged, and pregnant. Cast aside by her lover, the wealthy and spoiled scion of a Berks County family, she is forced into an arranged marriage to a man she barely knows. Adam MacPhail is a poor, ordinary iron worker whose dream is to become an iron master. Ellie's father, Stephen Bratton, well to do, well connected, and determined to save his daughter's reputation, orchestrates the union—not as Ellie would have it, but as he sees fit.

So begins a marriage in a time when a woman had no voice, no rights, no say in matters directly pertaining to her.

Ellie, exiled to the wilderness of Huntingdon County with a man she would not have considered three months before, declares her intention to make Adam's life miserable and make her father pay for his high-handed disregard for her rights.

Adam, unschooled in dealing with women, chooses to focus his energy and attention to turning a down-and-out iron furnace into a profitable, well-ordered producer.

Through the first half of the nineteenth century, on a self-sufficient plantation in the wilds of Western Pennsylvania, two people struggle to establish a life, disentangle an ill-conceived marriage, and make a success of a derelict furnace through the ups and downs of an unpredictable industry.

The Juniata Iron Trilogy
Book Two — Brothers

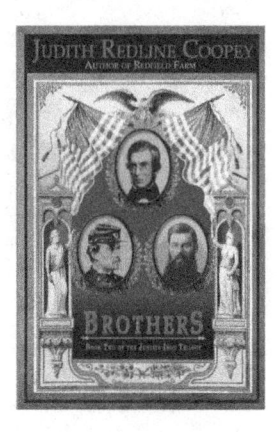

This second volume of the Juniata Iron Trilogy continues a family saga set against the nearly forgotten backdrop of Pennsylvania's 19th century iron industry. Laird MacPhail, son of the slain iron master at Etna Furnace, struggles to adapt to change: First the death of his father at the hands of an unknown murderer, then the realization that the mantle of responsibility for the whole iron plantation rests on his shoulders. Knowing that neither one of his brothers will take on the business, Laird puts away his dreams and gets to work.

But the country is in turmoil that will ultimately lead to war and suffering not yet imagined.

His brothers—Robert, who is handsome, charming and unreliable, and John, an idealistic, dedicated, solitary man—contrast with Laird's stolid, honest, hard-working ways.

Put them together and the MacPhail brothers make the consummate man. But taken one at a time, they struggle within themselves as the Civil War looms on the horizon.

Central to their world is the question of who killed their father. Suspicion centers on Jude Trethaway, son of Adam's lifelong menace, Simon Trethaway. But there is no proof of Jude's guilt, and it soon becomes apparent that he will get away with murder.